A Mediterranean Romance
The Capa Royals

E. Hughes

Love-LovePublishing, Madison, WI
ISBN: 978-1-961823-10-5
eBook ISBN: 978-1961823044
A Mediterranean Romance: The Capa Royals
E. Hughes. Available formats: eBook | Paperback distribution

Second Edition: 2024

Any resemblance to persons living or dead, as well as any location, event, or entity is purely coincidental. This novel is a work of fiction.

Other novels and works by E. Hughes:

Fiction:

Sixth Iteration
Disappear, Love
Business as Usual
Infatuation
A Mediterranean Romance: The Capa Royals
The Sapphire Chronicles: Broken Lair
Hello (A Screenplay)
Beyond the Plain (Poetry)
Digital Smiles (Poetry)

Children's Books:

Penelope Helps Mom and Dad
Penelope: Be Kind to Animals
Penelope: Super Duper Spectacular Princess Ballerina
Penelope: Don't be afraid
Penelope Holiday Cheer
Garden of Secrets

Nonfiction
Time and the Multi-Universe: A philosophy of time and time travel
Starting Your First Patio Garden: A Coffee Book
Family in a Time of Covid-19: The Truth about Coronavirus, How to Protect Yourself and Prepare
Reality Unbound (coming soon)

Chapter One

"What are you doing here? You're not supposed to see me before the wedding you doof!"

Marvin sat in a chair on the other side of our extravagant wedding suite and buried his face in his hands.

"I'm not sure that matters now," he answered, focusing his eyes on the carpet.

I strode across the room and twirled to show him how lovely I looked. For the first time in my life, I felt beautiful. With my big almond shaped eyes, high cheekbones, milky caramel complexion, and heart-shaped face, I was what most people considered attractive, not pretty. Or as Marvin would say, the prettiest girl in the world *to him*. We were supposed to get married at Chalet Terrace, the same place my parents were married forty years ago to the very day. Thank heavens I was only wearing a petticoat and not my wedding gown as I stopped before the vanity to fix errant strands of my perfectly coiffed hair. Wedding dress or not, it was still a jinx to see each other before exchanging vows.

"What do you mean, *'it doesn't matter now?'* Will you get out of here already? I have to finish my makeup and the girls will be back in a few minutes to help me into my dress. You're not even wearing your suit for goodness sake. You need to get dressed."

I was standing before him then, with both of my hands cupping his quivering cheeks. It was the most exciting day of our lives and Marvin was on the brink of a pre-wedding breakdown. His body shook and his lips were chalk-white, like he had just seen a ghost.

"I don't think you understand, honey…"

He finally met my inquisitive gaze, his dark handsomely sculpted face contorted into a combined look of anguish and guilt. He tugged my wrist and pulled me down to eye-level so that I was resting on my knee before him. For a moment I was more concerned about sullying the hem of my underskirt, than what he was about to tell me. He kissed me then gently stroked the back of my hair, "I can't do this."

"You can't do what?" I asked.

"I'm sorry, but… I can't marry you, Selena. I've been talking to Candace. She wants to get back together."

I felt like I had been kicked by a horse. *The hell was going on here?*

"And you tell me this an hour before we're supposed to walk down the aisle? How long has this been going on?"

"It started a week ago. She heard I was getting married and realized how much she missed me, how much she needed me."

"And she just figured this out three years after you broke it off with her?"

"—She broke it off with me."

"Is this your idea of a joke?"

"Of course not."

Despite his words, there wasn't a look of remorse on his face. I stood, numbly smoothing the wrinkles out of my crinoline underskirt, trying not to crumble as I floated back to the vanity. I then gazed over my shoulder at Marvin through our reflections in the mirror.

"So the past two and a half years meant absolutely nothing to you?"

"They meant everything to me," he pleaded.

"Then why are you doing this?" I bawled. A hot weave of tears plunged from the corner of my eyes, leaving a trail of mascara running down my cheeks. My shoulders collapsed as I heaved up and down in a succession of full-on sobs.

"How—could—(sob!)—you do this to me?" I wailed.

"I wouldn't think of hurting you like this unless it was absolutely unavoidable. I love you… I'm just not *in love* with you anymore."

He stood then, clenching his jaw.

"I'm sorry, Selena, but it's just the way it has to be."

My hands shook. I grabbed a hair brush and tried to brush my hair back in place.

"What am I supposed to tell people? That you walked out on me? Left me standing at the altar?"

"We never made it to the altar."

"Thanks to you!"

"Would you rather I had waited until after we were married? Until I had an affair or did something awful?"

"This isn't awful?"

"For both of us, yes. You were too good for me, Selena. I don't deserve you…"

"Damned right you don't."

I pulled my shoulders up, grabbed a handkerchief, and wiped my tear-stained face.

"You may have broken my heart, but you did not break *me*," I declared, pushing him aside.

Marvin reached into the interior pocket of his jacket and pulled out a slip of paper.

"What is this?" I asked.

"Tickets to Capa Isles, for what would have been our honeymoon. You take them."

"Thanks but no thanks."

I pushed him aside, damn near shoving him back into his chair as I strode to the closet, grabbed my suitcase, and stuffed my shoes, clothes and jewelry inside of it…everything except my $7,000, pearl white, crystal embroidered Vera Wang wedding gown. I wasn't sure what to do with it. I could leave it for hotel staff to dispose of, take it with me, toss it in the garbage or set it on fire. At the last second, I grabbed it, and stuffed it into one of my bags. It was too beautiful to throw away.

"Consider it a gift," he said, forcing the tickets into my luggage. "You deserve it."

I mentally sneered at Marvin's childish attempt to appease me.

"If it helps, I can tell everyone you left me," he offered.

I looked over my shoulder as I slid into a pair of jeans, and scoffed.

"So I can look like an asshole? I don't think so. Otherwise, tell them whatever you want, I don't care."

"It wasn't easy, coming here to do this. I wanted to run, but decided the decent thing to do is tell you to your face. I didn't expect you to be so immature about it. I was hoping we could handle the situation like adults."

"You actually have the balls to call *me* immature? You're scared…you were always scared to stand up and be a man. I should have known you wouldn't follow through."

Fully dressed in a t-shirt, a pair of old jeans and flip flops, exactly as I arrived to the bridal suite the night before, I hauled my suitcases to the door.

"I'm not the one running away. Relationships fall apart, Selena. You don't even have the *decency* to tell our family and friends what happened, do you?"

"That you dumped me an hour before the wedding? I think they'll understand if I don't. Have a nice life."

And with that, I marched out, closing the door behind me.

Chapter Two

The wind swept my hair into a state as I snuck through the back exit of the hotel to the busy sidewalk, sporting a pair of dark shades. The main entrance of the hotel was swarming with family, friends, and mutual acquaintances in town for the wedding. Marvin could deal with the fallout. He was the one who created this mess. It was a selfish choice, but under the circumstances who could blame me? I planned to send cards and thank you letters as soon as I was settled—anywhere but home. No phone calls, conversations, explanations, just a quick text to my parents to let them know where I was going. I just wanted to get away from Marvin, the prying eyes, the sympathetic stares, and the whispers sure to follow me the moment news of our canceled nuptials reached our family and friends.

Outside of the hotel, I raced to the curb and hailed a cab. Thankfully, the sidewalk was crowded so no one noticed me.

"Take me to the airport, please."

Concerned, the bearded, middle-aged Sikh driver peered at me through the rear-view mirror. "Is everything okay?" he asked, in a heavily accented voice.

"Everything is fine, thank you."

I was a mess with dry mascara running down my cheeks beneath a big dark smudge that appeared to give me a black eye. I pulled a compact mirror out of my purse and did what I could to repair the tear-stained damage to my face. Just because I felt like a disaster didn't mean I had to look like one. The forty-five minute ride to the airport gave me the time I needed to fix myself up. I might have finished sooner were it not for all the bumps on the road. Nevertheless, I was much improved, given the circumstances.

After our arrival at the airport, the kindly cabbie grabbed my luggage and hurled it onto a cart. I tipped him, and calmly walked through the airport pushing my belongings. Seeing as though this was my lucky day, I barely managed to get through airport security. I forgot to unwrap a wedding gift from my father and was pulled out of line for inspection.

The prickly security agent frowned her pudgy face. She was so small I could whistle and knock her over, but she had an attitude that was larger than the both of us. The woman pursed her lips and gestured for me to empty my carry-on bag.

"You know you're not supposed to bring a wrapped package through a security checkpoint. We need to inspect the contents."

"I'm so sorry," I stammered, "It was a wedding present, I forgot it was in my bag."

The day just kept getting better and better!

The security officer eyed my ring-less fingers.

"Don't people usually give gifts *after* the wedding?"

"I was supposed to get married this morning but my fiancé dumped me an hour before we were supposed to walk down the aisle. So here I am, off to my honeymoon alone."

"That's terrible," the woman said, shaking her head sympathetically.

"Don't worry, I've learned my lesson. It'll never happen to me again. As far as I'm concerned, men are dirtbags who will smile in your face while screwing another woman behind your back. For the first time in my life I plan to cry it out... then have some no strings attached fun!"

The woman's eyes softened.

"They're not all like that, honey…you just have to find the right one."

"Ah-huh, that's what they all say…"

I emptied my bag onto the table, scattering a tube of lipstick, tablet, a pair of underwear, jewelry, a book to read on flight, a hair dryer, bathing suit, tiara, wedding album, and a garter belt. As I proceeded to open the dreaded wedding gift, the security officer grimaced, waving a hand.

"Don't worry about the package ma'am. Have a safe trip."

"Thank you so much. I swear, I'm really *not* a terrorist."

"Please go."

I quickly shoved the contents of my carry-on back inside the bag and scrambled out of the room. My flight wasn't scheduled to leave for another 12 hours, long after what would have been our wedding reception, so I headed to the airline reservation desk to change my flight and hoped the clerk would be willing to adjust my departure without additional costs. I needed to get as far away as I possibly could, before the anger really settled in. Who in the hell was he to string me along for three damned years, knowing he wasn't over his ex? If he knew he was breaking up with me a week before the wedding, why didn't he do something about it then! I felt so humiliated.

I saved only a small amount of money for the trip to Capa Isles, just enough to enjoy a few meals and buy a couple of souvenirs. I lived on a modest salary, working as a city librarian. Marvin was the breadwinner in our relationship and was easily able to cover the cost of the trip, along with our hotel fees. In the end, I suppose he wasn't interested in marrying a librarian, especially when *the rat* had the option of sleeping with a dancer for the Charlotte Hornets.

It was three years ago, when a sweaty, insecure, three hundred and fifty pound man wobbled onto my floor at the city library in search of a diet book. I suggested his local weight watchers, but the successful businessman, ashamed of his weight, and the butt of many jokes at the office, wanted to lose weight discreetly. We discussed different types of diets and the many health books on our shelves that could help him well into the wee hours of the night…a conversation that eventually ended with an offer to help him lose weight. In the end, he decided the Atkins diet would be the best option because he could still eat meat. For a man like Marvin, carbohydrates were easier to part with. At the end of my shift, just as the library was closing, Marvin walked me to my car where he gently touched my hand and kissed me on the cheek. A few days later I invited him for a work out at the gym. Eighteen months later, and one hundred and eighty pounds lighter, we were in love.

****

"Hi, I'm Selena Capshaw. I need to change my ticket to an earlier flight."

"Is it economy, special, or business class?"

"Business class."

I gave her the ticket. The chipper squinty-eyed blonde typed something into her computer then made a face.

"I'm sorry ma'am, but your ticket is non-refundable, non-transferable, and changes must be made twenty-four hours before your flight."

"That can't be right, these are first-class tickets."

"Even if I made an exception for you, first-class is full."

"What about coach?"

"Economy is also full. I'm sorry…"

"Any other flight going to Capa Isles this afternoon? I'm desperate—I—I need to get out of here," I stammered.

One of my reasons for wanting to get away so desperately was fear that Marvin would come crawling back, begging my forgiveness. Another part of me was even more afraid that he wouldn't.

As I stood in line debating my situation with the clerk, a dark-haired man with handsome Mediterranean features glared at me from afar. I tried to ignore the stranger's mesmerizing gaze, but his piercing dark eyes drew me in.

"Unfortunately, the next flight to Capa is twelve hours from now," the clerk said.

I was grateful for the interruption. I looked away from the nosy stranger.

"If it helps, there's a hotel at the airport. We have a shuttle that drives by every half-hour that could pick you up."

"I'll give it some thought, thank you."

I walked back to the waiting area and sat down with a disappointed slump. I couldn't get to Capa yet, but I for damned sure, wasn't going back home. I needed space and time to reflect. Was I really that oblivious to Marvin's affair? Was I so engrossed in planning the wedding that I ignored the signs? Wait—why am I making this *my* fault? He's the cheater!

I fished around my bag for my phone and started emailing family members and friends.

A few minutes later I looked up to find the seductive Mediterranean stranger with the fiery dark eyes, standing before me.

"Please forgive the intrusion…I couldn't help but overhear your conversation."

From across the room it's called eavesdropping, I thought. He spoke in a thick accented voice.

I sucked my teeth. "Yeah, so?"

"I can help you."

"Unless you have a ticket to Capa, that won't be possible."

"Guess you are out of luck."

"Story of my life."

"What about a private jet?"

He sounded like Ricardo Montalbón from *Fantasy Island*.

"If I had a private plane I wouldn't be sitting here."

"What if I were willing to accommodate you?"

"Then I'm either really lucky or you're full of crap. I'm leaning towardss the latter."

He wore his dark, shiny hair slicked to the back, a tailored navy blue suit, and leather shoes that probably cost more than my entire wardrobe. He was not only drop-dead gorgeous, but had the most kissable lips I had ever seen. My heart palpitated. He stuck his hand out.

"My name is Andrasi."

I shook his hand.

"Selena Capshaw."

"Pleasure to meet you, Selena…see that gentleman near the exit in the blue suit and cap? That's Harold, my chauffeur. If you decide to fly

Air Andrasi," he smiled, "Harold will take you to my plane. We depart in an hour."

"No offense, Andrasi, but if you have a private jet, what are you doing here?"

"Waiting for my sister, Agnes. We will take the jet home to Capa when she arrives. In the meantime, Harold can drive us to my plane."

"Thank you, Andrasi. I deeply appreciate your help. Speaking of family, I should probably call my parents and tell them where I'm going."

Andrasi gave me a startled look. "Excuse me—but, are you of age?"

"Surely I don't look that young," I scoffed, though secretly flattered.

"You mentioned talking to your parents first."

"You didn't think I'd go trotting halfway across the world on a stranger's airplane without telling someone, did you?"

"Ah. Right. I apologize. That sounds like a very good plan." Andrasi extended an elbow. I linked my arm through his as the chauffeur grabbed my luggage.

"You seem like a very smart, very cautious woman. Your parents must be proud of you."

"I generally don't need their permission to travel. I just feel letting them know where I'm going is the responsible thing to do."

"Yes—it's not required, yet you do it anyway. Women aren't like that anymore. They long for independence."

"What's wrong with independence?"

"Nothing at all. I admire an independent woman. I longed for it myself when I was your age."

"Jeez—you make yourself sound so old. You don't look a day over thirty."

"And yet, I feel well beyond my years."

"You do have a world-weary look deep inside of your eyes," I smiled. "If you don't mind my asking?"

"Thirty-six," he smiled. "You?"

"Twenty-eight. I don't usually share my age or much of anything else with strangers, but since you were so open with me about yours, I'd feel bad if I didn't tell you."

Harold shuffled ahead with the luggage and carried it outside to a waiting car. He then held the door open for us and waited. The two of us climbed into the limo while he loaded my bags into the trunk.

"If you don't mind, I think I'll give my parents a ring now," I said, once firmly situated in Andrasi's car.

"I'll wait outside," he answered.

I called mother and told her where I was going and what I knew about Andrasi, which was just enough to track him down if something happened.

"I'm so sorry about the wedding, honey," mother said. "I can't believe Marvin would do this to you. Your dad and I adored him, but now, not so much after hurting my baby. How could a day so wonderful for me and your father turn out to be so unlucky for you?"

"Bad luck? After the way he treated me, I dodged a bullet."

"That's my girl, always seeing the positive."

"I apologize for not talking to you and dad in person. I was hurt and embarrassed."

"Don't worry about the rest of us. We'll be fine. I'll let everybody know that the wedding is off"

"Thanks, Mom. See you in a few weeks. We'll have dinner when I'm back in town."

"You bet," she answered, in that confident voice of hers.

I tapped on the window, signaling to Andrasi that I was ready to go. He poked his head into the car and my stomach flipped. In that short amount of time, I'd forgotten how gorgeous he was.

"Done?"

"Yes, thank you," I answered, swiftly looking away.

He smiled, as if reading my thoughts, then climbed in. He was probably used to women fawning all over him.

We drove to the private airport runway in silence, the both of us checking our smart phones, when Andrasi suddenly tapped the glass partition separating us from the driver.

"My sister has arrived. Please get our guest aboard then return to the airport terminal to retrieve my sister," he said to the driver.

"Yes, boss," Harold answered.

He parked the limo next to a Bombardier BD-700 Global Express, a renowned luxury plane for jet setting billionaires. Harold hopped out of the car, opened the door, and escorted us to a pair of comely twenty-something year old flight attendants who then led us to the plane. The interior, which had been sectioned off into separate cabins, was even more opulent than the sleek silver exterior.

The first cabin was all white, with a white leather and gold trimmed sofa, white leather recliners for the regular seating areas, a large movie screen, thick white carpeting, a well stocked bar, and white marble dining tables. The second cabin was a spacious all white bedroom, the next bedroom featured a round bed covered in a lavish all white, fur blanket (faux I hoped), like something out of a James Bond movie. The fourth cabin was a full-sized kitchen with a chef. The fifth cabin was an office with tinted glass floors with a view of the main bedroom. Andrasi's plane was fit for a king.

"Wow, these are some digs," I said.

"If you're going to travel across the world, might as well do it in style."

"And you've got plenty of it."

At this, he smiled.

Andrasi escorted me to the sofa and gestured for me to sit down.

"And what part of the world are we traveling from?" I asked.

He smiled. "From Capa."

"Ah, a native... so, are you in town for business or pleasure?"

"A little of both," he said, offering a devious grin. "I'm here to see an investor friend about naturally, some investments he wanted to tell me about.

"Oh," was all I said.

I accepted a Cosmopolitan from a bubbly dark-haired flight attendant.

"Investing in anything special?"

He stared at me for a moment.

"You could say that..." he offered flippantly. "The investor buddy I was supposed to meet never showed up. He sent me a text, however," Andrasi shrugged his muscular shoulders.

"How rude, I'm sorry."

He waved a hand.

"Well, I suspect something went wrong. The flight was a surprise for his wife. They were to vacation in Capa."

The attendant poured Chardonnay into Andrasi's glass.

"She would have been pleased."

"And you?"

"It's lovely, very comfortable."

The dark-haired flight attendant appeared again.

"Sir, your sister is here."

"Terrific, thank you Lori," then looking at me, "If you'll excuse me…"

Andrasi left, moving from the main cabin to the exit. As I watched his departing figure I wondered, *"Who is he?"* Was this his plane or was he the high-ranking employee of someone extremely powerful? Powerful men don't fly to foreign countries for the sole purpose of collecting an investor, let alone offer rides to random women at the airport along the way. Andrasi was the point man for someone very important.

I was snapped out of my thoughts by the distant sound of my cell phone ringing. I looked at the caller I.D. It was my best friend and maid-of-honor, Tiffany. I figured I had better answer her call before takeoff.

"Girl! You're going to Capa by yourself? All that paradise and no honeymoon…at least you get to ride on a private plane. Is he cute?"

"Gorgeous, actually."

"He sounds like he's interested in you."

"Doesn't matter, because I'm not interested in *him*. The only thing I'm interested in is having some fun…something I've denied myself for too long. The plane is nice, I just wish you was here. Takeoff is in a few minutes, his sister just arrived," I whispered.

"You don't have to wish, I'll go to Capa with you!"

"Tiffany, *please*… you don't have to do that, I'll be fine."

"Glad for ya, but we can be fine together. I could use a vacation and some time with my best friend. You shouldn't be alone on your honeymoon."

"It's not a honeymoon anymore. What about work?"

"I'm part-time, sweetie."

"I would leave the tickets with Harold but Marvin's tickets are non-transferable."

"That's okay, I'll buy my own."

"On a part-time salary?"

"Girl please, I have my ways."

"Ways" meant she would get money for tickets from one of her wealthy boyfriends.

"Fine. I'm staying at the Grand Agnes Hotel on Capa Bay."

"Alright Boo, I'll start packing. Maybe I'll meet some cute guys out there," she giggled.

By *cute* she meant, *wealthy*. To Tiffany, there was no one uglier than a man with a low balance in his bank account.

However, knowing Tiffany was coming to Capa with me immediately put my mind at ease. I couldn't wait to see her. She was trouble, big trouble…which was exactly what I needed. We met four years ago when I hired her as a library assistant for my floor at the city library. She was fresh out of college, where she majored in fashion design. Day after day, as we labeled and restocked books, I'd listen to stories about her exploits and rendezvous with wealthy men. She drove an expensive car, lived in a lavish uptown apartment, and wore designer clothes on a salary barely above minimum wage. She didn't need a job at the library. She worked there because it gave her something to do. Tiffany was the girl I wanted to be. The girl who had fun. The girl who *never* got her heart broken.

When Andrasi returned twenty minutes later, the flight had already taken off. I expected to meet his sister, but she was tired, and had already retreated to one of the cabins to rest. I finished my Cosmopolitan and moved from the table to a white leather recliner next to a window. Andrasi sat in an adjacent chair, and gazed out at the clouds billowing around the plane.

"Agnes sends her apologies. She was tired and needed to rest."

"Your sister doesn't know me from a can of paint, so no worries."

"In Capa, it is considered rude not to greet our guests."

"The more you talk about your country, the more I think I'll like it."

"I certainly hope so."

He sat back, fingers intertwined, his eyes beaming with pride.

"You are so proud of your country… aren't you? We don't see that very often where I'm from. People complain when we have so much to be thankful for. It's refreshing to meet someone who truly appreciates where he's from."

"We take great pride in our nation."

"What do you do for a living?" I asked.

"Tourism policy, trade, investments and many other things that would bore you if I went into detail."

"The tourism part sounds like fun, and definitely explains this tricked out plane. So, as the official tourism specialist, what do you recommend I do for fun when I get to Capa?"

"I can think of a few things," Andrasi answered, smiling devilishly.

I rolled my eyes. "Oh whatever! Seriously, I'm traveling across the world alone, and I need things to do!"

"Even I have to admit that going alone isn't as much fun. May I ask what happened?"

"I'd rather not talk about that," I answered, clamping my lips together. I turned and gazed out the window at the cloudy blue sky.

"Forgive me, I didn't mean to intrude."

He smiled, as if it would melt the glacier forming between us.

"I would start with sightseeing. We have fantastic olive orchards and wine vineyards for tourists to explore. Caves, beaches, and one of the tallest waterfalls in the world. There are always lavish parties to attend, if you can acquire an invitation. There are also plenty of wonderful places to shop."

I looked up and grinned. "The only thing I can afford is window shopping."

"Our stores are not so expensive so I'm certain something can be arranged."

"That won't be necessary. I have plenty of new dresses to wear."

"Ah, but how are we going to boost the economy if tourists don't shop or spend money?"

"Good point. *Fine*…I promise to spend money while visiting Capa. Happy now?" I raised my hands in mock surrender.

"The people of Capa thank you."

"The people at my credit card company will probably thank me even more."

He gazed at me from under a veil of thick dark lashes and tapped the hand rest of his chair nervously.

"You're very beautiful," he observed.

"Thank you," I answered, sheepishly. "I'm not used to being called beautiful."

"What else would they call you? Stunning? Gorgeous? Lovely?"

"You're being silly," I laughed.

He leaned forward and gripped my hand.

"Why? I've never seen a woman as stunning as you in my entire life."

I raised a hand. "Seriously, stop!" I laughed. "You're embarrassing me!"

"I'm not joking."

I drew my hand away and looked out the window again.

"What do you do for a living?" Andrasi asked.

"I told you before, I'm a librarian."

"A modest profession for a very modest woman."

"I don't usually look like this, today was supposed to be *my*…" I took a deep breath. "I'm only like this because of my trip to Capa."

"Today must have been a very big day for you."

"Yes. It was."

"May I ask how a woman as attractive as you, can seem so surprised that a man finds you attractive? Is it that you go out of your way to look plain or that you are too modest to accept a compliment?"

"Not exactly. I just happen to think a lot of women today rely on their looks instead of intelligence or wit. They think being beautiful will give them a free pass but they're taking the easy way out. They want to be like reality TV stars, the wives or girlfriends of athletes, or celebrities."

"And you don't?"

"Of course not!" I replied, cheeks warming. "I pride myself on going to work every day, and earning my own way. It's true, that beautiful people are treated better in society, but I know my looks didn't pay my way in life. I did that on my own. Besides, not everyone gets to be beautiful, so how is that fair?"

"Kind of the same as someone who's born rich. It's not fair to the rest of the world, but it happens. May I ask what your parents do for a living?"

"Jeez, I feel like I'm being vetted for the presidency. My father owns a couple of grocery stores, and my mother is a homemaker."

"You're so ordinary..." Andrasi replied, his eyes lighting up, "It's fascinating."

"Gee, *thanks*."

"No, I mean that in a good way. I meet celebrities, politicians, religious figures, billionaire executives and clientele. These are people who believe they are the exception, that they're special and deserve to be treated better than everyone else because they're famous. The ones who expect to be treated like royalty have five or six assistants to wait on them hand and foot. It's refreshing to meet someone who embraces normalcy, and derives from it a sense of dignity and pride. What do you do for fun, Selena?"

"This might sound boring but, I like to read. That's why I work at the library."

"You're unreal," he said, waving a flight attendant over to pour him another glass of chardonnay. "Everyone likes to read. What else do you like?"

"Oh whatever. I like everything normal people like. Dining out, traveling, fashion, oh, and gardening…"

"Ah, now we're getting somewhere."

"What about you? What do you do for fun?" I asked.

Andrasi half-smiled. "Do I strike you as the kind of man who has fun?"

"Sure. You seem like the adventurous type, like someone who gets excited at the idea of doing something new."

"Trust me, it's hard to get excited when you've seen the world twice over."

His voice was suddenly heavy with disappointment and regret haunted his shimmering dark eyes. The last thing I needed was to spend the next few hours with someone more depressed than I was, so I tried to lighten the mood.

"You were excited a few moments ago," I beamed, poking him in the chest.

Andrasi leaned across the seat and caressed my arm with his fingertips, making me shiver from head to toe.

"Beautiful women always excite me."

I tried to think of something clever to say in return, but my mind went blank. The brush of his fingers against my skin was electrifying.

Andrasi cupped my chin, lifting my face so that I stared him directly in the eyes.

"...And there is nothing more exciting to me than experiencing life with someone who is seeing the world for the first time."

Without breaking my gaze, I moved Andrasi's hand away from my face. It was still my wedding day, even if my heart had been broken. He caressed my cheek with the back of his fingers as he drew his hand away, which left me quivering from my head to the tips of my toes. Sensing my unease, Andrasi released me.

"I've taken up enough of your time..." he abruptly stated. "The bedroom is down the hall. If you get tired, feel free to use the master cabin as you see fit. Enjoy the rest of your trip."

When he spoke, his lips were a breath away from mine. I felt an overwhelming desire to brush the hair away from his perfectly sculpted face and kiss him.

Ahem. *Marvin who?*

Andrasi rose from his seat and I managed to stammer a polite "thank you," as he strode away.

Despite my cool exterior, on the inside, I felt like I had been turned upside down. If Andrasi intended to join me in his cabin, then he was sorely mistaken. There was no denying it, Andrasi was a good looking man, but I was still very much in love with Marvin. Was he expecting some sort of payment in return for the flight? If so, I would pay him back in full, even if it meant depleting my savings or paying him back over time even though Andrasi didn't exactly strike me as the type of man who would accept layaway.

After I was certain Andrasi was out of earshot, I put a pair of headphones on and listened to airplane music, which played Puccini's *Madam Butterfly*. *Too sad,* I thought. I needed something that would lift me up so I immediately clicked the next song on the playlist, O *Mio Babbino Caro,* before finally turning it off. So much for getting him out of my head. Clearly, Andrasi had a flair for the dramatic.

Luckily, he didn't come back which allowed me to relax and enjoy airplane's grandeur. I spent the next two hours reading then enjoyed a glass of *Château Latour* red wine and a gourmet meal cooked by Andrasi's chef, while watching an action movie with Harrison Ford about a terrorist group hijacking an airplane. Exhausted by the events of the day, and with another three hours of flight to spare, I crept down the hall to the all white cabin bedroom, quietly passing the staircase to Andrasi's office, kicked my shoes off and fell asleep. A short while later, a flight attendant shook me awake, prompting me to return my seat to put my seat belt on. We had arrived at Capa International Airport. After landing, three comely young flight attendants unceremoniously ushered me off of Andrasi's luxury private jet into a waiting car, a silver-colored Maybach driven by Harold, his abiding chauffeur. I felt a twinge of disappointment. I was hoping to thank Andrasi once again for allowing me to travel on his plane, but he failed to emerge from his office. I wondered, with some regret, if the ladies had another flight or if he simply wanted me gone. Knowing someone on this faraway exotic island had given me some comfort, but alas, the man had already washed his hands of me.

I thought nothing more of my surreal experience with Andrasi as I watched the scenery of startling blue oceans, white sand beaches, cabins, and cottages pass by. Instead, I contemplated what my honeymoon would have been like and how Marvin and I would have spent our time together as newlyweds. Tears stung the corner of my eyes but I refused to let them fall, especially with Harold peeking through the rearview mirror. I clasped my hands together and stared at the floor until the tears subsided. The car came to a halt and Harold hopped out and opened the door.

"We're here Miss Capshaw. Can I do anything else for you?"

"Thanks, Harold, I'm fine. Did you enjoy your trip?"

He smiled sheepishly.

"I enjoyed the trip very much, ma'm. The plane is exquisite," he said.

"Just call me Selena. I'm in Capa for two weeks so I'm sure we'll cross paths again."

"Thanks, Selena. I'd like that."

Harold carried my bags into the Grand Agnes Hotel and left them with the bellboy while I was attended to at the front desk. The clerk was a tallish man with a Greek accent similar to Andrasi's. He was sharply dressed in a berry and gold colored hotel uniform, and matching hat, with his gelled back, jet-black hair curled beneath it. He wasn't as clean-shaven or as clean-cut as the hotel clerks I was used to seeing in America. He was distinctly masculine with a no-nonsense demeanor as he ignored the incessantly ringing telephone in favor of focusing of me as if I were the most important person on the planet.

"Miss Capshaw, I presume?" My name is Nicolai, and I am the manager of the Grand Agnes Hotel. Welcome to Capa! I sincerely hope you enjoy your stay with us. Here are the keys to your room."

Nicolai slid the receipt and keycard across the desk with aplomb. There was no mention of Marvin when he was the one who arranged for the trip and paid for our suite, so how did Nicolai know my name much less recognize my face? The brusque manager snapped his fingers and a bellboy swiftly pushed my luggage over to the front desk.

"Take Miss Capshaw's belongings up to our luxurious Capa Suite. And please, Miss Capshaw, enjoy a bottle of Chateau Latour red wine, courtesy of the Grand Agnes Hotel."

Did he just say *Capa Suite*? Brochures on the counter of the front desk displayed pictures of the hotel's most extravagant room...a two level suite with a wraparound veranda and an astounding view of the oceanside. According to the receipt, the room was priced at $12,000 USD a night. I pushed the keycard back to Nicolai.

"I can't accept this."

"Is something wrong?"

"My fiancé's travel agent booked a smaller hotel room."

"Your room was upgraded courtesy of the *Prigkipas, Andrasi*—"

The phone at the front desk rang, but it was not a typical ring. This one had a special tone,

one that stiffened Nicolai's back and made him stand with his shoulders straight. He grabbed the receiver swiftly then snapped his fingers at the bellboy, speaking in a clipped, urgent tone.

"Please show Miss Capshaw to her room, I must take this."

Without waiting for a response Nicolai put the phone to his ear and turned his back.

I wondered what could be so important to make him treat a guest so dismissively. Unwilling to debate him further about the room, I collected the keycard and the receipt, and followed the bellboy to the elevator. The only thing I wanted at this point was a bed, didn't matter to me if it was a single or double.

With the elevators closing around us, I was looking forward to a few hours sleep before starting the rest of my trip.

"Have you been to Capa before?" the bellboy asked, his eyes alight with curiosity.

"No, first time," I answered.

"First time for everything at least once, huh? You're American, aren't you?"

"Yes, why do you ask?"

"I can tell by the way you're dressed. I like America. I went there with my grandparents when I was little. Capa is the smallest city on the planet. I can't wait to travel the world on my someday."

"Trust me, Capa's hardly the smallest city on the planet. We have towns in America that are much smaller than Capa."

"Really? It looks so much bigger on TV. America's the first place I'm going to. New York," he answered, matter-of-factly.

"*Cool.* New York can be expensive so save as much money as you can for the trip."

"I'm not worried, I've got more than enough money," the young man drawled, "but my grandparents won't let me go. The name's Gavin, by the way."

The elevator stopped. Gavin slid a keycard into a slot and the elevator doors opened to the Capa Suite. The first thing I saw was a foyer twice the size of my living room, marble floors, a crystal and gold chandelier the size of a bath tub, and a breathtaking view of the oceanside.

"Amazing!" I gasped over my shoulder, as I walked inside. I inhaled the beauteous scent of fresh roses emanating from a bouquet left on a marble accent table near the door. I pulled the card from the side of the vase, expecting a generic message from management:

"Hope you are enjoying your stay in our beautiful city – See you soon, Andrasi."

After leaving my luggage in the foyer, Gavin departed from the room unnoticed.

"See you soon?" Had Andrasi made arrangements with Nicolai while I was in route to the hotel? Was he planning to visit?

My heart thundered in my chest and the adrenaline in my veins raced like a horse at the Kentucky Derby.

I paced to the living room and looked around. A staircase in the center of the room led upstairs to a loft where the main bedroom was located. I glanced around the corner. There was another bedroom just down the hall.

After peeking inside, I ran up the stairs. The first thing I did was open the doors to the veranda, allowing a fresh ocean breeze into the room. The declining sun had cast a red orange hue onto a staircase that led to a private beach from the wraparound veranda. I ripped my shirt off, slid out of my pants, and raked my hands through the now tangled tendrils of my hair as I walked outside. I ran downstairs and let my bare feet sink into cool white Mediterranean sand. Marvin would be here, had he chosen not to abandon me on our wedding day. Maybe not in the Capa Suite, but somewhere in this hotel in another beautiful room. So much beauty wasted on such a terrible day.

I let the grief sink in and the tears roll down my cheeks as I strolled the beach alone, the wind lifting my dark brown hair. As the waves rolled onto shore and twilight settled in, I reveled in the seclusion of the private beach. I could wail as loudly as I wanted and no one could hear me. I collapsed to my knees then lay on my stomach, my cheek against the sand. The moon brought a heavy tide. I allowed it to wash over me, soaking my silky black camisole and creamy mocha skin in salty sea water. With my eyes closed I sighed deeply as the breeze caressed my face. If I only could start the day anew, wake up in my bed back home… and that awful conversation with Marvin at the hotel before the wedding never happened...today would still be my wedding day, and Marvin and I would get married and live happily ever after.

I finally awoke to the tender warmth of a hand on my shoulder. *"Marvin?"*

He shook his head slowly. With the light eclipsing his figure, his face was merely a shadow.

By then, the moon had settled high in the sky. Its luminous light beamed down on my head.

The night breeze, and its companion the sea, left goose-bumps along my chilled skin. The hand rubbed until my arm was warm as I placed my open hands over my face and wept.

"We were worried about you," Andrasi said. "Concierge knocked on your door. Your clothes were strewn on the floor and we couldn't find you. You could have gotten hypothermia out here in the water for so long."

I heard genuine worry in his voice. He drew me into his arms and pressed my face against his chest.

"What are you doing here?" I asked.

"I could ask the same of you," he gently, chided.

"I felt like crying."

"You can cry inside. You shouldn't be out here."

One of my tears trickled down to his hand. Andrasi took his shirt off and wrapped it around me.

My teeth chattered. "I'm so cold."

"Let me take you inside."

He slid an arm under my leg.

"No, I can manage—"

Ignoring my protests, Andrasi scooped me into his arms and draped my arm over his neck. I felt the wind beneath me as he silently carried me across the sand, up the stairs through the veranda, to the master bedroom.

A small night-light flickered on by sensor as we stumbled inside. Andrasi released me to the big comfy hotel bed then disappeared. I thought nothing, I felt nothing but numbness as the trauma of the day—getting jilted at the altar finally sunk in. Andrasi thankfully returned a minute or so later, seating himself on the edge of the bed with a small glass of scotch.

"This will warm you up," he said, cupping my cold wet hands around the glass.

I took a sip of the liquor, which burned on the way down my throat. Andrasi smiled. "You'll get used to it. It's very old, and very strong."

After taking another sip I passed him the glass and laid my head on one of the big feathery pillows. He brushed my hair away from my temples then gingerly kissed my forehead. In the darkness, his night-shaded eyes sparkled in the shimmering moonlight.

"I didn't want to say anything before, but…" he hesitated, taking a deep breath.

"But what?" I asked.

"About how beautiful you are. You are the most beautiful woman I've ever seen. On the plane I couldn't stand to be near you, but I couldn't stand to be away from you either. I'm not used to having these feelings, especially for a woman I just met. I did my best to avoid you for the rest of the trip but I can't stay away. I'm sorry."

We were strangers, but the energy emanating between us in the darkness made us feel intimately familiar.

"You're lying," I said.

"But you are—

I put my fingers over his lips. "You were going to say something else, weren't you?"

"What makes you say that?" he asked.

"You paused like you were about to tell me something but realized it wasn't the right time or the right thing to say."

"And you think what I told you just now was any easier to spit out?"

"It had to be or you wouldn't have said it."

"Doesn't make it any less true."

"Is that why you looked for me?"

Andrasi rubbed a hand through the back of his hair like he was frustrated. "You were right. I came here to tell you something, but realized it doesn't matter, so…"

I sat up. I was curious now.

"What is it?" I asked.

He shook his head.

"Like I said, it doesn't matter now. May I see you tomorrow?"

He interlocked his fingers between mine.

"For what? I'm sure you'll see me around town, here and there."

"For dinner. We're friends, right?"

"Well… I suppose. You did save my life."

At this, Andrasi smiled.

"And you saved mine."

He leaned forward and kissed me, his lips consuming mine until I was breathless. His hands roamed my flesh as he pressed every inch of his male physique against my soft, acquiescing form. I moaned faintly, closing my eyes as he wedged his hips between my thighs and his fingers caressed my budding nipples. He groaned, then in an act of gentlemanly restraint, quickly drew away. "Get some rest, okay?"

The timbre of his voice caressed my skin like silk.

I nodded, hoping he would leave before something regrettable happened as I turned on my side, towardss the moonlight streaming in through the windows.

"Goodnight…" I finally answered, barely turning to look over my shoulder.

I felt his presence vacate the room as I closed my eyes.

Chapter Three

Simmering heat and blinding sunshine filtered into my suite through the open veranda doors. I climbed out of bed. It took a moment for the haze of sleep to wear off before I remembered where I was. Every inch of the room had been covered with big bright beautiful bouquets of flowers. I smelled a pink rose and blushed, my head swirling with memories of my encounter with Andrasi. *What was I thinking, making out with a complete stranger?*

I plucked the petals and scattered them all over the bed. My pillows still smelled like his expensive cologne. I suddenly squealed with girlish excitement, then rolled out of bed with a thud. *Why wouldn't I make out with a handsome stranger?* I'd always been responsible and what did it get me? Jilted at the altar. *I promised to have some fun on my vacation, so why not?*

The housekeeper who had been in my room in the early hours of the morning had picked up last night's mess in addition to arranging the flowers. The cheerful housekeeper was also likely responsible for the onslaught of sunlight permeating the room. I could hear her in the dining room, singing over the noisy vacuum—which by itself, was loud enough to raise the dead.

I walked downstairs, forsaking the cozy comfort of the loft bedroom for something to eat. *Why was I still so tired?* Must be jetlag.

The maid, who looked to be around fifty or so wore headphones and danced as she cleaned. Sensing my presence the woman turned the vacuum off and draped the headphones around her bony neck. She was thin, almost frail with big poofy black hair.

"It's about time, sleepyhead! It should be a crime to sleep so late in Capa!"

"Oh," was all I said, as she fluffed the pillows and swept the back of the sofa with a colorful feather duster.

"You look like I just slapped you across the face," she smiled. "What would you like for breakfast?"

"Oh—no, you don't have to do that."

The woman chuckled. "The chef has already arrived. You'll eat whether you like it or not."

Where I came from, there was a line—and staff didn't cross it, especially when interacting with hotel guests. But I kinda liked not having to deal with the normal formalities...as long as she didn't get *too* nosy.

"My name is Daniella," the woman said.

"Are you from Capa?" I asked.

"Born and raised. I'm a dark, fiery, hot-blooded, Capian woman."

"Indeed you are," I observed.

The woman cackled.

"Does that surprise you? Americans are always shocked by how direct some of us are. We're like family around here -so don't mind us, especially any folks with sharp tongues. You'll get used it... *in time.*"

"I won't be here long enough to get used to it. I'm leaving in two weeks."

"*Strange...*" the woman mused. "I was under the impression you'd be staying longer. The *Prigkipas* is very smitten with you."

I sighed. She was definitely one of the nosy ones.

"Andrasi's feelings have nothing to do with my future plans."

"The *Prigkipas* always gets what he wants, especially when it comes to women."

"Then he's in for a disappointment."

She shrugged her bony shoulders.

"Will you be here at the suite every morning?" I asked.

"I'm at your beck and call for eight hours a day everyday for the next two weeks. Of course, there's nothing to do around here, unless you're a sloppy little piglet."

"Well, you don't have to worry about that," I assured her.

"Great. Then we'll get along just fine. It'll make it that much easier for me to keep the suite perfect for the *Prigkipas*."

Before I could get a word in edgewise to ask what '*Prigkipas*' meant, Daniella continued…

"For what it's worth," she added, "you'll hardly know I'm here." Then after a pause… "I can see why he likes you. You look like that woman, the *Magdalena*."

"Danni! Please leave that poor woman alone, she's here to relax!" a heavy, American sounding voice called from the kitchen.

Looking like she'd been busted saying or doing something she wasn't supposed to do, Daniella put a finger to her lips and "shushed me" guiltily.

A tall, bald, heavy-set man in a white chef's uniform walked into the dining room where Daniella and I were talking and nudged her with his elbow.

"She's a guest, act like you have some sense, woman!"

"This is that gal the *Prigkipas* is so crazy about," she said.

"Hi, I'm Selena. You must be our illustrious chef?"

"My name's Dave. Nice to meet you," he said, staring at me with an amazed look on his face.

I shook his extended hand.

"See, the resemblance is uncanny, isn't it?" Daniella said.

"I wasn't expecting to stay in such an extravagant suite, let alone one that's fully staffed. I was supposed to stay in one of the smaller rooms."

"No, no no, that wouldn't be proper at all," Daniella replied.

Before I could ask Daniella why, Dave, with a threatening look, pulled her into the kitchen.

It would have been easier to dine out or cook something myself at this rate, which I had no problem with, of course. The last thing I needed was a maid or a chef. Who are these people who can't pick up their shoes or wash their own plates and need a full-time staff?

As I turned to go upstairs, Dave and Daniella's hushed voices filtered into the room, the two of them suddenly making a commotion as they stumbled back into the dining area. Dave carried a tray of fruits, vegetables and cheese that had been fashioned into a bouquet of flowers, and Daniella carried a tray of bread, biscuits and butter, which she balanced on one of her arms, while carrying pitchers of orange juice and water on the other. After setting the table, Dave arranged the food, leaving Daniella to pour water into one of the glasses. "Would you like some OJ?" she inquired.

"Yes, please. This is way too much food for one person to eat. Would the two of you care to join me?"

Such a beautiful setting, and there I was, about to sit and eat it all alone...instead of with my groom.

"I'd love to, but I'm on the clock," Danni answered. "Besides, *the Prigkipas* will be arriving soon. Everything must be perfect."

"I've got sausages simmering, I'll be in the kitchen," Dave said, making a hasty break for the other room.

"The *Prigkipas?*"

"The *Prigkipas, Andrasi*. Yes, he was here an hour ago. I told him you were still asleep."

"Did he say why he was here?"

"Why would he? It's his room."

And with that, she walked out, joining Dave in the kitchen.

My heart raced. The upgraded room and the private plane came with strings attached, just as I suspected. I had been in such a state the night before, I didn't question how Andrasi had gained access to the room and the private beach.

My emotions spiraled out of control, from feelings of anger to total confusion. Just who in the hell did Andrasi think he was, inserting himself into my life and vacation in this manner? He took advantage of me when I was vulnerable, pretending to be a gentleman when he clearly had other intentions. Accepting the plane ride from Andrasi had been a mistake. Accepting the lavish hotel suite had been a mistake. Allowing him to carry me off to bed and making out with him had also been a mistake, and I had no one to blame but myself. How in the hell was I going to extricate myself from this situation with no money?

I should have known better than to accept extravagant gifts from a stranger. After all, what on earth could he possibly want *aside from the obvious and why did he want it with me, of all people*? Well…it was time to find out. If there was one thing I *wasn't* afraid of in my life, it was confrontation.

I was still boiling with anger and still ready for a fight twenty minutes later when the bell rang and Daniella went bounding to the door to let him in. She held the elevator button, her gaze averted, head lowered deferentially, as he strolled inside. Maybe it was the manner in which Daniella's back went stiff and her shoulders went straight as he passed her by that bothered me. He looked taller than I remembered…his dark gaze more hypnotic and sensual, his shoulders broader, and his arms and chest more defined with rippling muscles. A quiver ran down my spine and popped between my thighs.

A pair of nondescript men dressed in dark suits stalled in the foyer behind him until Andrasi waved them off, casually sending them back onto the elevator. After a swift scan of the room, the men left. They too, had seemed overly officious. Was Andrasi a politician? He had a presence, an air about him that commanded deference, unlike the humble, passionate, man who had cared for me the night before. The mood in the room shifted as he strode to the table to sit down. Daniella, who had been relaxed minutes before now walked around as if on egg shells. Before Andrasi's butt could touch his seat, she was already at the table with a kettle, pouring a cup of tea, which was served in pricey Royal Albert dinnerware.

I sat at the dining room table with my crossed leg bouncing up and down as I picked at one of the melons on my plate with a fork distractedly.

"Good morning, beautiful. Mind if I join you?" Andrasi asked, as he sat on the other side of the table and helped himself to a piece of fruit.

"It's your suite, so why are you asking me?"

Sensing the tension between us, Daniella abandoned the room. Andrasi popped a grape into his mouth before finally looking up.

"Yes, but it is polite to ask because you are my guest."

"I'm on vacation and I was supposed to be a guest at this hotel."

"*My hotel,* which makes you *my* guest."

"Since when?" I spat, dropping my fork on the plate. "What's your angle, Andrasi? Because I'm starting to feel like you orchestrated this entire thing from the moment you invited me on your plane."

"Does that include your fiancé jilting you on your wedding day?"

My eyes instantly swelled with tears. "How did you know about my wedding? And how dare you throw it in my face like that!"

Andrasi sighed. "I'm sorry. I shouldn't have blurted it out that way. When I offered you a ride on my plane, I was trying to be helpful. When we met, I told you I was in town to meet an investor. That investor was your ex-fiancé, who happens to be a good friend of mine. The luxury plane trip was a wedding gift.

Unfortunately, he told me the marriage was off at the last minute. When I saw you moping around the airport I recognized you immediately. I knew you were his former bride."

"Did he invite you to the wedding?"

"Of course. In fact, I saw you at the hotel. That's how I recognized you."

"Goodness…I'm so embarrassed."

"Why? There's nothing to feel ashamed of. Friend or not, I would say Marvin's the one who behaved like a jackass."

"You let me carry on like everything was okay when you knew the entire time! And what kind of friend kisses his friend's former fiancé?"

I rose from my seat at the table and walked across the room.

"I apologize for making you feel uncomfortable. When I saw you at the airport my heart went out to you. You looked so vulnerable and alone. I was just trying to help, in my own way. As for the rest, who could resist? You're not his fiancé anymore, so why should he care? I only invited you to my hotel suite because I wanted to help."

I felt a hand on my shoulder turning me around.

"Why do I feel like your *help* comes with strings attached?" I scoffed.

Andrasi cupped my chin, lifting my face so that I stared directly into his eyes. "Because it does," he answered, lowering his eyes. "The only thing I want in return for my kindness, is to make you happy."

"Why?"

"Because it's what I do. Now…I will leave you to enjoy the rest of your day. You promised to have dinner with me and I'm holding you to it. I will return tomorrow at 5 pm to pick you up. I also extended a line of credit for you at Blue Royal Boutique. We will be attending a very nice, very upscale place for a dinner party. All of the movers and shakers in Capa will be there so feel free to have your hair done, get a massage, a manicure…the works."

I crossed my arms over my chest.

"Unlike everything else in your life, I'm not for sale. You can't buy me, Andrasi, I don't care how rich you are."

"And that's exactly why I like you," he said with a smirk. "This is for you to wear to the party."

Andrasi reached into his pocket, retrieving a jewelry box containing a ruby necklace interwoven with intricate strands of gold between the stones. The necklace was paired with a set of matching earrings.

"Andrasi..." I gasped. "This is too much, far too extravagant and much too beautiful for me... I have nothing remotely appropriate to wear with this. I can't accept it, I'm sorry."

Andrasi took my hand and slipped to his knee. "You are wrong, Selena. These jewels may be extravagant, but they pale in comparison to your dazzling beauty and radiant eyes. Here in Capa, my love, you will discover yourself to be the princess you truly are."

Then he was up on his feet again while I stood there with my mouth agape, trying to conjure up a response. When Andrasi referred to me as *'my love'* it was probably just a Mediterranean thing, just as giving me the 'princess' treatment was Andrasi's attempt to promote his beautiful country. But what did he hope to gain from lavishing me with expensive gifts? Someone famous would be a more appropriate target for this sort of promotion. My friends were regular people and would never have money to visit a luxurious country like Capa.

"Are you alright? You look seasick," Andrasi said.

"I'm a little uncomfortable with you wasting all of this...*luxury* on me."

"You're driving me crazy, you know that? This is all for you, *my love*.... Now, please go out and see the city, it's a beautiful time of year.

Harold will take you wherever you wish to go. I will see you tomorrow at six. Okay?"

"Thanks but no thank you. I'll travel just like any other tourist. Besides, the Blue Royal Boutique is in the hotel shopping area, right?"

"Yes, just downstairs."

He leaned forward and kissed me gently on the forehead. *"Tomorrow…"* was his final word.

With Andrasi finally out of my hair, I was able to sneak in a few hours touring the city. Capa was a distinct blend of Spanish, Italian and Greek culture, with almost too many rules to keep track of. The streets were clean, the people were polite, but as Daniella mentioned, outspoken. Some of them had even pointed at the foreigner trolling their streets, or stopped to stare directly at me. *"Magdalena!"* a woman exclaimed, pointing and laughing as I walked by.

Despite its wealth, the small Mediterranean country had a meager population of 150,000 citizens in a country two hundred miles wide. Yet crowds of locals and visitors quietly toured the bustling ancient city or made use of its green-blue sea and white sand shores. It was hard not to get lost with so many people swarming about. The streets were also too similarly named… Capa Lane, Capa Drive, Capa

Terrace…streets I learned had been named after the Island's royal family, whom the locals affectionately referred to as the Capa Royals. There was to be a party at their estate tomorrow, and I wondered, if it was the same party Andrasi had invited me to. It was likely that a man of Andrasi's stature was acquainted if not directly employed by the royal family.

After some time on the beach collecting sea shells, I went to dinner where I was served a light dish at a Mediterranean restaurant where I ate sautéed eggplant, figs and olives with pasta, in basil sauce. It was odd being alone in a foreign country. I was used to dining out and eating by myself at home. In New York, you never really feel alone when you have the beat of the city to keep you company. I was grateful when Andrasi and his security detail strolled into the restaurant, half-way through my meal.

"Mind if I join you?" he asked.

I looked up to find his handsomely dark face staring down at me. I slurped a half-eaten noodle into my mouth and gestured for him to sit. There was a clamoring and shifting of seats as people turned to look, which did not surprise me, considering his reputation in Capa. Still, I found their pointing fingers, whispers, and side glances unnerving.

"Do people in Capa always point and leer at foreigners?"

"Only the beautiful ones."

He flashed a smile.

"It's disconcerting. I feel like I have something in my teeth. What are you doing here?"

"If I'm not mistaken, this *is* a restaurant."

He lifted a brow.

"Sorry—it didn't occur to me that you'd have reason to eat near the hotel."

"Actually, I don't. I was looking for you," Andrasi answered.

"Oh," was all I said, in response.

"I know you're on vacation but, I was hoping you could take a look at my family's library. I'm willing to pay you."

The waiter appeared at the table and took Andrasi's order. I bit into a fig. His security detail, which comprised of three men, dawdled casually near the door. A woman rose from her seat and tried to approach our table, but one of the men stopped her mid-way, directing her back to her table.

"I would be happy to," I said. "I've always had an interest in estate libraries."

Andrasi placed his hand on top of mine. His eyes were full of warmth and unexpected tenderness.

"Good. I was hoping you would say that."

I tried not to squirm as I slid my hand away to pick at my food. *Why did he have to be so handsome?*

"What are you hoping to accomplish?" I asked.

"Order. We use a very old filing system. I'm hoping to bring you in as a consultant who will update us to the cataloguing system you use in the States."

"Sounds easy enough, and would be a great project for my portfolio."

"Terrific. You will be an enormous help to our curator, who is at his wit's end. I'll have a contract drafted and delivered to you tomorrow."

"Perfect. This will give me something to do. I'm only a day and half in and I'm already bored."

"Bored? You don't like it here?"

"No, it's beautiful…great, actually. Just lonely. I wasn't expecting to be here by myself."

"You're not by yourself," he answered gently, holding my gaze.

Then, as if snapping out of a trance, he gestured for the waiter and ordered a glass of wine. A jazz band played on stage. The singer of the band sounded like an Italian Harry Connick Jr. Sensing that I was enjoying the music, Andrasi stuck his hand out.

"Would you like to dance?"

"*No*. I'm a *terrible* dancer."

"I doubt it. Are you always this difficult?"

"Most of the time."

He rose from his chair, grabbed my hand, and pulled me out of my seat. Onlookers turned and stared at us with amused expressions on their faces as he led me to the small black and white checkered dance floor.

"I'll lead," Andrasi whispered in my ear in response to my bemused sigh.

The music played by the band picked up, and Andrasi spun me around. My skirt twirled and blew upward from the draft. I whooped in surprise, which seemed to further amuse our audience.

Of course, Andrasi was an excellent dancer, and I'd taken ballroom dancing lessons at a community college a few summers ago. A few songs in, I was actually having fun, despite being out of breath and tired. I laughed more than I had in months at my clumsy missteps and Andrasi's attempt to overcompensate for my shortcomings on the dance floor. He was better than good, he was superb. But of course, he was the kind of man who had the money, time, and breeding to not only learn how to dance but to accomplish anything he set out to do.

Eventually the tempo of the music slowed and we found ourselves cheek to cheek, my eyes closed, with Andrasi's hand pressed on the curve of my back. When I opened them the restaurant was empty and dimly lit. Only the waiters remained as they slowly cleared dishes from the now empty tables. I suddenly imaged myself with Marvin and felt a wave of sadness. When the band wrapped for the night, we left and Andrasi walked me back to the hotel. We took the elevator to the Capa Suite. The doors opened and he walked me inside.

"This is where we say goodnight…" I said, after a few moments of awkward silence. His security detail watched from the foyer as we walked to the living room.

"Unfortunately," he grinned.

He leaned forward and kissed me, then boarded the elevator with his guards, after wishing me a good night.

The next day I went to the Blue Royal Boutique to have my makeup, hair and nails done as planned. There, I was first greeted by a woman who was barely out of her teens. Her flimsy blouse, pants and earrings were neon pink, and looked like they had been purchased out of a mall gift shop. Like most teens, she went for the casually-messy look, with her sloppy dark brown hair piled on the top of her head, eyeliner that looked like it had been drawn on by a thick black pen, and low riding jogging pants that barely covered her non-existent derriere.

"Hi, my name is Ana, welcome to Blue Royal Boutique. Please remove your clothes and take one of the white terry-cloth towels from out of the cabinets," she demanded, making very little eye contact.

"When you're done, follow the circles on the floor to the massage station. The masseuse will massage your face, then the rest of your body. We promised the *Prigkipas* we would take good care of you," she smiled, while dumping a pile of hot steamy bath towels into a waiting basket.

"May I ask how much this is going to cost?" I inquired.

The girl shrugged.

"Beats me. The bill has already been taken care of. Enjoy your stay," she recited.

"Okay..."

I followed the young woman's instructions, stripping out of my clothes into a terry cloth towel and bathrobe in an all white changing area. I then stuffed my belongings in the assigned locker and followed the circles on the floor to the next station where I was greeted by a man in his twenties. He was deeply tanned with long blonde hair and wore a white tank top and butt-hugging white shorts, like a 1970s gigolo. I tried not to giggle at his appearance as I flopped on the massage table, wearing only a white towel. The young man quickly went about his business, working my sore muscles into a state of relaxation that left me so limp I was practically drooling on the massage table. When he was done, I put my robe back on, stiffened my wobbly knees and walked to the hairstyling booth. There, an attractive, stylish woman in her forties escorted me to a sink where she washed my hair.

"So…" she said, just as she was finishing up, "you are a friend of the *Prigkipas*, yes?"

"I suppose…" I answered, as she brought my head from under the water. My ears popped as she towel dried my hair and led me to a styling booth.

"I'm not sure what the *Prigkipas* means, but…"

The woman laughed. "You have no idea? I suppose he means to keep it that way so I won't spoil the surprise."

My interest was piqued. *"Surprise?"* I asked.

I tried turning in my seat to look at her.

"Oh, never mind," she answered, waving a dismissive hand. *The Prigkipas* is a nice man. He and I were friends, once. You get used to the lifestyle he provides then one day it goes away when he tires of you. Then you have to get used to being normal again. I suppose it was all for the best or I may not have met my wonderful husband," she mused.

"I see. So is that how he operates?"

The woman, blithely ignoring my question, turned the hair dryer on.

"You have a lovely face. You look like the *Magdalena*."

"So I hear," I replied, wondering still, who this Magdalena was. I didn't ask for fear of looking like an uncultured oaf.

"I suppose I have no business saying that. It's taboo. The Magdalena was beautiful. Enchanting, like you."

The stylist leaned back and stared at my face. "Very, V*alley of the Dolls*. This hairstyle is chic. Very stylish," she boasted, lifting her chin as she observed my face and hair.

The hair-do was nice, but much higher than I was used to. I tried not to pat the bouffant down as the hairstylist ushered me off to the makeup chair where I sat for an hour while the makeup artist plucked and arched my eyebrows, darkened my eyelids and lashes, and plied blush to my cheeks. After painting my lips, I had my nails and toes manicured. When I was done, I was given a bag containing my clothes and sent back upstairs to the Capa Suite wearing only a pair of fuzzy slippers and a plush terry cloth towel. People stared at me as I walked through the lobby, some of them with their mouths open. I felt beautiful in a way that made me self-conscious. I wasn't used to being stared at in *that* way. Even on my wedding day, as I charted an escape through the busy hotel and made my way to the airport, no one noticed me. But here they were, hotel busboys, business men, and even couples holding hands stood slack-jawed as I slithered by. I was grateful when the private elevator arrived to take me back to the Capa Suite. Once inside, I leaned against the wall and sighed. What a day!

The first thing I saw when I walked in was the contract to work on Andrasi's family library. The undersigned (me), would agree to work for an amount that was three times my salary back home. Without bothering to read the rest of the print, I signed the document and left it on the table for the courier.

Realizing it was already 5 pm and I still hadn't decided on what to wear, I raced upstairs to the master bedroom, ruminating over the unremarkable state of my wardrobe. That's when I noticed when the gold colored gift box waiting on the bed for me.

I sighed as I kicked my shoes off and drew my feet onto the bed. My curiosity piqued, I swiftly opened the package and removed the tissue paper. Inside of the box, there was a beautiful red dress with shimmering embellishments. I removed the satin garment and splayed it across the bed. It was a spaghetti strapped slip dress, with a diamond cutout back. I ran my fingers along the smooth luxurious fabric.

'What is Andrasi up to now?' I groaned. There was also a shoebox at the foot of the bed with a note on top.

"A beautiful dress for a beautiful woman…

– Andrasi" …the note read.

The inside of the shoebox contained a pair of Valentino heels.

The sound of the doorbell ringing nearly startled me out of my senses. I looked over the railing at the living room to see Daniella heading towards the door. Had Andrasi already arrived? It was only 5:15.

"Miss, there is someone at the door for you, a young woman."

"Let her in, please."

A minute later I squealed and raced downstairs where I was met with open arms and a look of surprise judging from Tiffany's wide open mouth.

"I can't believe you're already here," I exclaimed, as the two of us embraced.

"WOW, you look fantastic!" she squealed.

I spun around.

"Do I? I just had my hair and makeup done." I touched the back of my hair self-consciously.

"Honey, you look great! Not that there was anything wrong before, but you're just…so stunning!" Her lashes fluttered in disbelief as she spoke.

"I know it's a little over the top for me but…"

"No explanations required. You deserve to treat yourself. Are you going somewhere?"

"Oh," I answered, remembering Andrasi. "I have a date."

"A date!" she exclaimed. "That was fast! I'm shocked, but in a good way! I feared you would be sitting around, brooding about Marvin, that's why I rushed out here. I wasn't about to let you stay by yourself in some foreign country. I'm so happy for you."

Tiffany had not only been a great friend, but no matter what, she always had my back.

"My moping and brooding days are over. For the first time in my life I'm actually having some fun. But this man is so generous, I don't know what to do with him. He insists on buying me things I don't want or need. But, now that you're here, I can't leave you and go to some party."

"Who said you had to leave me?" Tiffany smiled.

"Aren't you tired from the flight?"

"A well-traveled woman never gets jet-lagged, my dear. Now, tell me more about this wonderful man and this party you're going to."

"Well, it's invitation only and apparently very high brow."

"Hmmm lots of wealthy men I suppose."

I rolled my eyes.

"*Married,* wealthy men, so don't even think about it."

"I didn't come here to ruin your plans, so you're going to the party with or without me. We'll catch up when you get back," she said, softly patting my arm.

"I'll ask Andrasi if you can come. I won't enjoy myself knowing you're here alone. Did you bring a dress? He'll be here at six."

Daniella led Tiffany to the other bedroom as I returned to the master suite to get dressed. With only a half-hour left before Andrasi was to arrive, I quickly slid into my elegant red dress and heels, then stood before the mirror and appraised the results. For the first time in my life I felt…*perfect.* But deep inside, the situation felt so wrong. I was supposed to be a married woman. I was supposed to be on my honeymoon with the man I fell in love with… but fate decided it was not to be.

"Wow. You're not just going to the ball, you're the belle of the ball. You look great!" Tiffany exclaimed as she walked into the room, fully dressed in a stark white mini-dress, five inch heels, big gold earrings, and a gold plated necklace bearing her name. She was dressed like a true Jersey girl. But Tiffany was tall, leggy, and had the bone structure of a Victoria Secrets model, which allowed her to get away with wearing scanty outfits to classy parties, usually on the arm of some rich old fool.

"So do you," I beamed. "At least it didn't take a three-hour makeover to do it."

Tiffany rolled her eyes. "You were gorgeous before the makeover, hun."

I gave her a skeptical look as I sat on the bed and put my ruby earrings in.

"I'm not like you. Men don't fall over themselves for me."

Tiffany put her hands on her hips and scoffed like she was fed up.

"Because you have no confidence in yourself! I'm serious, Selena. Stop beating yourself up. You're beautiful. What he did to you was inexcusable. Whenever you have a fight with Marvin, you get depressed and start putting yourself down. I'm sick of it."

I stared in wide-eyed disbelief at my friend. "Do I really act like that?"

"*Yes,* you do!" she answered, in an admonishing tone.

I couldn't believe Tiffany traveled halfway across the world to yell at me.

"I'm not really that pathetic, am I?"

"You're not pathetic at all," she sighed. "Just heartbroken, and who can blame you? You have a wonderful man who wants to spend time with you right here in Capa. Marvin wasn't right for you. I hated the way he treated you."

Tiffany was right. We were happy and very much in love until he lost weight, looked in the mirror and saw a set of six-pack abs for the first time in his life. Then our relationship took a turn for the worse when he realized women were starting to notice him, not only for his good looks and newly toned physique, but his expanding wealth. Marvin was slated by business magazines and news articles as the next Warren Buffet. *I was good for him, damn it!* But what did Marvin ever do for me? He was intelligent, sweet, and self-effacing in the beginning. I was the one who encouraged him to open his own investment firm. I was the one who accompanied him to dinner parties where I helped schmooze hard-to-win clients. He couldn't believe his luck, he'd said to me one day, and now he believes that I'm the one who should be grateful to have been with someone like him? Marvin wouldn't be the man he is today without me!

"You're right. I deserved better than that. I'm not wasting another moment of my time on this beautiful island, thinking about Marvin. I do love the man, but I'm also completely over him."

"The love part will end in due time," Tiffany assured me. "Falling in love is easy. Digging yourself out of the rubble is the hard part."

The doorbell rang. I checked my cell phone. It was just after six o'clock. A few seconds later, Daniella appeared on the stairs.

"The *Prigkipas* is here."

Tiffany gave me a quizzical look. "The *Prigkipas*?"

"I've been trying to figure that one out myself," I shrugged.

Daniella's lips curled into an amused smile as she turned and walked down the stairs. I adjusted my clothes, checked my makeup then followed her to the living room, with Tiffany descending after me a few seconds later.

Andrasi and three men who looked like they were part of a security detail waited in the foyer. I could see what all the local fuss was about when it came to the *Prigkipas*. He was tall, dark, and damned sexy, in a tailored navy blue suit with various pins and medals covering his masculine chest. My toes curled in my shoes as I remembered the sensuous warmth of his lips brushing across mine, the strength of his muscular arms as he carried me from the beach, and the tenderness of his touch as he gently laid me to bed. Andrasi exuded an air of cool that no man could match, as he leaned against the wall with his lithe legs crossed at the ankles, hands shoved into the pockets of a pair of slim-fitting suit pants that left nothing to the imagination. He casually surveyed the suite through a veil of thick dark lashes, his dark eyes absorbing every detail as I descended the spiral staircase into the living room. His mouth parted a little when he saw me, but stopped short of speaking when he noticed Tiffany coming down the stairs behind me. I continued walking until I was within an inch of Andrasi. The scent of his cologne was intoxicating. I managed to keep my composure as he leaned close and whispered sweetly into my ear.

"You look beautiful tonight…" he said, tracing a finger down my arm so gently it gave me goose bumps.

'Thank you…" I stammered. "I should have mentioned this before, but I invited my best friend to Capa after the…you know, the break up."

Andrasi smiled over my shoulder at Tiffany. "We're going to a dinner party. Would you care to join us?"

He extended an elbow, which Tiffany happily accepted while mouthing, "Gorgeous!" behind his back as she took his other arm.

Outside, we were quickly divided into separate vehicles, with me and Andrasi riding with Harold in a silver Maybach and Tiffany riding with Andrasi's security detail in a separate limo.

"You don't mind, do you?"

Judging from the goofy look on Tiffany's face, she was more than fine.

I nodded as he took my hand and led me into the car.

"Let's take the other route, shall we?" Andrasi said to the driver after we'd scooted into our seats.

"You got it, boss..."

At Andrasi's behest, Harold took the scenic route to the party, which was along a stretch of road that provided a picturesque view of the country's cliff sides, elaborate landscapes and more of its white sand beaches. A blanket of stars carpeted the sky as the sun began to set beyond an amber horizon. Andrasi tucked his chin into the curve of my neck and gazed over my shoulder as I took in the passing scenery, which consisted of hilly grape vineyards and a span of olive orchards that seemed to go on forever. He nuzzled the side of my neck like a horny teenage boy.

"The tour bus missed the most important part of the country. Who cares about the tourist areas? This is the side of Capa that I wanted to see."

"If you weren't so damned stubborn you could have seen it yesterday. There was no convincing you to let Harold take you on a tour. I can arrange for you and your friend to go on a hike tomorrow, if you're interested."

"Tiffany's not the hiking type."

"Then I'll go with you," Andrasi offered, entwining his fingers between mine.

Our eyes connected as he stroked the back of my hand with his fingertips. He then nestled me into the crook of his arms, which encircled my waist as he toyed with my hands from behind.

"You've probably seen it a thousand times. I can't ask you to do that."

"I haven't seen it with *you,*" he answered.

I tried not to blush. I looked away, directing my attention back to the passing scenery.

"I would like that," I answered, quietly. "By the way, thank you for the spa and the beautiful clothes."

"My pleasure," Andrasi grinned, looking quite pleased with himself. "We're dining with Capa's most elite family tonight."

"Capa's most elite family? What does that mean?"

"It means we're dining with the royal family," he answered brusquely.

Suddenly my hand was free as he turned his attention to the window on his side of the car.

"I was hoping you wouldn't say that…"

This got Andrasi's attention…he turned and stared at me with the most dumbfounded expression in his dark eyes.

"Care to elaborate? Most women—*no,* most people would give their left arm to dine with the royal family."

"I'm not most people," I answered.

"Indeed, you are not."

"No offense, but spending time with the royal family isn't exactly my cup of tea. It's intimidating! There are so many formalities involved I'd worry constantly about embarrassing myself. I couldn't imagine having to deal with such a tight-knit, high status family all the time. Do you visit often?"

"Often enough," Andrasi shrugged.

"You don't seem too happy about it, which gives me the impression that hanging out with the royals isn't at the top of your favorite list of things to do either."

"Having you with me more than makes up for it."

Andrasi kissed the back of my hand. My arms went as limp as noodles. Then something outside of the car caught my attention. In the middle of a field stood a cross the size of a skyscraper. It was barely a blur as we sped by.

"What was that I asked?"

"What was what?" Andrasi answered.

"That big structure out in the middle of the field?"

"A cross. It was built sometime in the medieval era. A gift from Rome."

"Wow…" I gasped. "I'd love to see it."

Andrasi laughed. "You really do amaze me, you know that?"

"Why?" I asked, confused by his reaction.

"You would rather see a thousand year old structure than have dinner with the royal family. You were completely unfazed when I told you where we were going."

"Oh."

He leaned in.

"Selena…you really are an amazing woman."

He caressed my fingers once more. As if on cue, the partition separating us from the driver closed. I sighed as I closed my eyes and Andrasi's lips found mine. The kiss was passionate, yet achingly tender even as his hand pushed against my spine, crushing my chest against his. My hands roamed every inch of his tense physique. He left a trail of kisses down the curve of my neck to the swell of my cleavage as the soft satin gown gave way and slipped from my shoulder revealing the silky slip beneath.

"I've wanted to do that from the moment I first saw you."

"The first time you saw me I was with my fiancé," I panted, trying to regroup as I straightened out my disheveled dress and errant tendrils of my hair.

"I know…and I would have stolen you right from under him if given a chance."

"I wouldn't have let you."

The sparkle in Andrasi's eyes flickered deviously in the dull light.

"Provided, you had a choice."

"There's always a choice, Andrasi. I choose the man I want to be with, not the other way around."

"That's not what I meant," Andrasi said, his hand resting on my cheek as the pad of his thumb caressed my lips.

I was spellbound by the intensity of his fiery gaze as he spoke.

"If destiny has its say, the two of us are meant to be."

A knock on the back passenger window broke the spell. I was so enraptured, I didn't notice when the car stopped in the circular driveway of a massive castle.

Suddenly, my heart no longer fluttered because of Andrasi, but out of fear of meeting the royal family. What was the proper way to greet the king or queen for that matter? Do I curtsey or shake their hands? How traditional were they? Or had they become somewhat modernized? Andrasi must have read my thoughts. He patted my shoulder consolingly.

"You'll be fine," he assured me.

"This is the palace?"

"No. It's a castle. A palace is in the city, a castle is in the country. The royals reside in the city during the colder months and certain holidays. When you meet the King and Queen, don't curtsey or shake their hands. Simply nod your head as a means of acknowledging them when you're introduced. And calm down, I can see your heart beating through your chest," he smiled.

"I'm sorry, it's just a little nerve-wracking, that's all. You dropped this on me at the last second."

Harold pulled the door open and I climbed out of the vehicle. Andrasi joined me a few seconds later and offered me his arm as we walked to the door. Tiffany arrived in the limo a few minutes later, but was too far behind to enter the party with us.

"Should we wait for Tiffany?"

"No. It would be improper for me to arrive with two women on my arms. I will have her announced when she arrives. The family will be happy to receive her as my guest. By the way, the press is here. This part of the dinner is a highly formal event."

"What is the occasion?"

"My brother has formerly accepted the crown."

Chapter Four

I would have fallen flat on my face as we walked into the royal family's castle, if not for Andrasi's synaptic-like reflexes, which saved me from an embarrassing tumble on the ground. I'm unsure if my knees gave way or if I simply blacked out from pure shock.

"Are you okay?" he asked.

"*No,* I am not okay. I'm stunned. Is that what all of that *Prigkipas* business was about?"

This also explained his security detail, the extravagant plane, and the deference he was shown by staff at the hotel.

Andrasi linked his elbow into mine as we entered the foyer. I surveyed the room, which had floors and pillars that were made of marble with intricate strands of gold woven into the design. The decorative flooring led all the way up to the second floor of an elaborate spiral staircase to a long hallway that lead to numerous bedrooms. This section of the castle was referred to as the Queen's quarters, though occasionally referred to as the Queen's apartments. The chandelier hovering above the staircase was large like the one at the Agnes Hotel, but elegant and tasteful. The walls were covered in paintings of the royal family in different eras going back as early as the medieval period. The paintings employed several styles that included Macedonian, Byzantine, and Renaissance artwork. The building was primarily built of limestone and marble in the style of ancient Greece, which made the interior of the castle cool and airy, even during hot summer months.

"How could you keep this from me?"

"I didn't keep it from you," he uttered between his teeth while grinning at guests as we passed them by. "I assumed you would have figured it out on your own by now."

The first paparazzi appeared. An overweight man with thick brown hair, a grizzly looking beard, in a t-shirt and baseball cap snapped our picture. The camera's flash made my eyes flutter.

"Prince Andrasi, care to tell us about your guest? Who are you wearing?" he asked, shifting his attention to me.

I'd already forgotten who the designer was. The photographer sounded American… definitely a tabloid or entertainment journalist.

Andrasi ignored the question, but acknowledged the man with a slight nod of his dark head.

"You just *assumed* I would eventually figure this out? I don't speak the language, Andrasi. I can't read the signs or your newspapers for that matter. You should have told me. I don't want my photo in the paper or anywhere else!"

"Too late for that," he drawled, as another photographer appeared before us and snapped our photo. I was never one to read the tabloids, so I was unfamiliar with the Capa Royals. But it appeared they were of interest to the public, much like other royal families. I felt a smug sense of satisfaction wondering what Marvin would think when photos reached newspapers at home. "This is beyond rude."

"It's life."

"*You're* life," I snapped. "I happen to value my privacy."

"I'm sorry—I should have said something but I wanted you to get to know me for who I am, not *what* I am."

"Deception of any kind is unacceptable. Especially given the situation I had to deal with back home."

Andrasi turned to face me mid-step. "I wasn't trying to deceive you. I'm sorry—please forgive me, my beautiful Selena."

He held my hand within his and another photographer snapped our photo, making me cringe.

"I forgive you, but this is the first and last time. Do *not* lie to me again… even by omission."

"You have my word. I do solemnly swear I will never lie to you ever again, from this day forward and for all eternity. The past is the past, right?"

I wiped my hands together.

"It's in the past."

"Good. Let's start over from here. We were having such a good time. I'd hate to see it ruined by this."

"As would I…" I replied, surprised by my own admission.

After walking down endless candle-lit corridors covered with wall to wall paintings of past and present royal family members and free standing columns sculpted, many of them during the Renaissance era, we entered a section of the castle where the state rooms were quartered. Guests of the royal family mingled and lingered about while a staff of prim and proper servants dressed in black suits and white on white shirts and ties, served champagne, Carpaccio, and Salmon Tartare hors d'oeuvres on gold platters. Nearby, the Queen's dining room was attached. The room consisted of dramatic Victorian era furnishings, drapes, Greek statues, and more paintings of the royal family, set in gold frames. The dining table was long, stretching from one end of the massive dining hall to the other, and could easily seat over one hundred people. The tables were covered with white table cloths, and had more silverware per person than I could count.

Andrasi looped my elbow through his extended arm.

"Don't' worry, just do whatever I do."

"You have a knack for reading my thoughts, don't you?" I said.

"I wish I knew what was going on in that stubborn head of yours!" Andrasi laughed.

Doors to the adjoining dining room opened and a servant appeared.

"Would you mind if introduced you to my parents?"

I followed his gaze across the room past a line of guards in red suits holding antiquated rifles, to a seventy year-old man and an elegant seventy-ish woman with black and silver-streaked hair. She wore a strapless, burgundy, floor-length ball gown with a diamond the size of a small boulder around her neck.

"Are you sure?" I asked, meeting his cooler-than-calm gaze. My stomach was in knots.

"I've never been so sure of anything in my life," Andrasi answered.

I followed him across the room to his parents—the King and the Queen.

"May I approach, your Highness?"

"You know you needn't ask," the Queen responded, smiling warmly.

The royal guards parted like the Red Sea, allowing us through. Andrasi hugged his mother then stood back as she looked him up and down.

"Are you eating well? You look thin."

The expression in her eyes was tender and motherly.

"I'm fine, Mum. And you? Are you well?"

"Keeping us all on our toes, as usual," the King chimed in.

Andrasi smiled. "You're supposed to be taking it easy. I thought your trouble-making days were over…"

"Not by a long shot," the Queen answered, with a wink. "I've got some years left in me yet…even with your brother assuming the throne next year."

Her sharp hazel-eyed gaze shifted from Andrasi's face to mine, a look of recognition flickering in her eyes.

"Mum, Dad, meet Selena Capshaw. Selena, meet my Mum, Antonia, and my father,

Giovanni, the King and Queen. "Selena will be working with our curator updating the library to a new system."

I remembered Andrasi's instructions on how to greet the royal family.

"I'm honored to meet you," I answered, with a slight nod of my head.

"Thank you," the woman said, tightening her lips. "It's nice to finally meet one of Andrasi's friends. Where are you from?"

Her tone was disapproving.

"New York," I answered.

"I thought I detected an East Coast accent. I lived in New York as a child," the Queen continued. It was a lovely place, at the time."

"It has its charms," I answered.

"And you're one of them." Andrasi responded, draping an arm over my shoulder.

"She is *something*," the Queen grumbled, before turning her attention back to Giovanni. "Shall we eat?"

Giovanni extended an elbow. Antonia accepted then gestured for the party to proceed. The Royal Guards cleared a path to the dining room and a procession of dinner guests followed the Capa Royals inside. Within minutes, everyone was seated, with Andrasi three seats away from the King. I was placed across from Andrasi on the other side of the table. I felt a twinge of disappointment upon realizing we wouldn't be sitting together. I looked up to find Tiffany flopping into the chair beside me. I'd almost forgotten she was here. A second later, a man with a deep olive complexion, long dark hair, and mysterious ocean blue eyes sauntered in and sat next to the King.

A furtive looked passed between Tiffany and the man who had just walked in behind her.

"Where were you?" I whispered to Tiffany, a few seconds later.

"The Queen's apartments."

"What exactly, were you doing in the Queen's apartment?"

"Having some fun! You're not the only one who can bag a prince."

I shushed her. The Queen was sitting right next to us.

"I don't care about that."

"I do," Tiffany beamed.

"Who is he?"

"*Stavros,* the crown prince, silly!"

"You met him?" The look on my face was incredulous.

Tiffany adjusted her slightly wrinkled dress and smirked. Stavros sat to the right of the King, followed by Giovanni the III, who was second in line, Andrasi, who was third in line for the throne, and finally, his sister Agnes, who was fourth in line for the throne.

"I'm famished!" Tiffany exclaimed. "If I don't get some food I'm gonna start eating the table cloth."

I stole a glimpse down the table where I saw the flash of a camera from a member of the press. Journalists camped outside of the room peered into the doorway at the royal dinner. The Queen cut a disapproving look at Tiffany.

"Save your appetite and words for the after party," the Queen whispered in my ear. "The royal family doesn't engage in small talk in front of the press."

But I wasn't a member of the royal family. Were guests of the prince not permitted to speak?

"I apologize for any impropriety on my part, Your Highness."

The Queen blinked, her lips curling into a sardonic smile.

'Miss, whatever your designs on this family may be, do not think I am buying this doe-eyed act of yours for a moment. My son may have fallen for it, but I won't."

I glanced across the table at Andrasi. He seemed to be enjoying himself as he talked to his father and brothers, and thankfully had not noticed my exchange with the queen.

"You can rest assured, my designs on this family goes no further than this dinner and designing your family's library."

The Queen gave a nod of approval then stoically turned to accept a dish from one of the servants. After the first course was served, a photographer entered and took pictures of the royal family and their immediate guests. I observed their detached hands-in-lap pose and followed suit, while Tiffany smiled for the cameras like she was taking a selfie and threw in a peace sign for good measure.

"This is boring," she finally said. "And this soup is whack."

She tossed her spoon on the table.

"Act like you got some sense, we're eating with the royal family," I muttered.

"You said we were going to a party, not a royal funeral...sheesh!"

"Apparently, there is an after-party and if you don't cut it out, you won't get an invite. Besides, that 6'6 royal guard looks like he's about to throw you out on your narrow ass."

Tiffany feigned a yawn, drained the wine in her glass, then signaled for another. After her third glass, she pointed to a painting on the wall.

"I'd like to propose a toast… to my friend Selena, a spitting image of that woman in the medieval painting," she slurred. "How'd you get up there?" she giggled.

The main photographer snapped my picture, then a photo of the painting. The name beneath the work of art, which had been engraved in an elegant script read, *Magdalena*. For a moment, everyone at the table was dead silent as they gawked at the image then back to my face. Suddenly, there was a chattering among the press and a flurry of flashbulbs went off. The King and Queen, poised as ever, were careful not to utter a word or so much as glance at the painting, which made me curious about who the woman in the painting was.

I managed to make it through the rest of the dinner without embarrassing myself, despite frequent outbursts from Tiffany about everything from how old and gaudy the castle was, to drunkenly asking the Queen her age.

With all of the craziness surrounding Andrasi's family, I'd all but forgotten about Marvin. My wedding and the life I left behind at home was starting to feel like a distant memory. I felt a strange connection to Capa—like I belonged here.

Aside from occasional eye contact at dinner, there was little opportunity to talk to Andrasi and I was actually starting to miss him. I was grateful when the royal family was ushered into a private room, leaving the public and the press behind. All who remained of the party were fifteen to twenty friends and members of the immediate family, who sat to eat in a cool but cozy den next to a crackling fireplace in a dark, rustic room.

The couples walked out of the dining room arm in arm, in a procession, down a corridor to the after-party. I clung to Andrasi, while Tiffany walked arm in arm with Stavros, to the queen's surprise and bemusement. I watched, with some amusement as the horrified look in her eyes turned to rage.

Otherwise, the family was in a relaxed mood, with the King picking hors d'oeuvres from a tray on a nearby table and the queen lounging near the fireplace with Stavros, Andrasi, and Agnes. Giovanni the III hid near a darkened corner, whispering with a great degree of secrecy on his cell phone, every now and then turning to look over his shoulder to see if anyone was watching.

The private social gathering was near the Queen's Garden, a beautiful oasis encircling the west wing of the castle, complete with a moat, a beautiful array of flowers, rows of olive and apple trees, pools, grotto, and sparkling waterfalls, surrounded by a green elaborate maze covering a few acres of land.

"Stavros, I'd like you to meet Selena. She'll be working on the family's library with the curator," Andrasi said, formally introducing me to his older brother.

"Pleasure to meet you, Your Highness."

"Stavros." He extended a hand. "We don't do any of that highfalutin crap behind closed doors," he barked.

Tiffany, who was already off her ass drunk, drained a glass of champagne then stumbled over to the prince rolling her hips.

"Hey Prince Charming…wanna dance?"

She smiled, showing too much teeth. Despite his good looks, Stavros was anything but charming. He came across as petulant and rude. He slid an arm around her waist as if to steady her.

"I see you and Tiffany are already well acquainted," Andrasi noted.

"Yeah. Thanks," Stavros replied, with a devious grin.

"I think she could use a cup or two of coffee," I offered.

I draped Tiffany's arm over my shoulder and escorted her to a nearby chair, where she would be out of the Queen's sight but within earshot of the brothers.

"My kind of girl…not only does she know how to party, she doesn't take life too seriously, either. I adore her," Stavros exclaimed.

"Don't get too carried away with your feelings. You'll be married soon."

"Not if I have anything to say about it. I'm not interested in any of mother's high-born, mono-browed arranged brides. When I'm king, no royal born male will be subjected to an arranged marriage ever again. It will be my first decree."

"The king's role is to uphold the very tradition you forsake, brother."

"I'll marry any woman of my choosing. Even her," he said, gesturing in Tiffany's direction. "Now if you'll excuse me, I have some drinking to do," he sneered.

We left the brothers in the den. After escorting Tiffany to a quiet room, I plied her with food and coffee, hoping she would come to. She went in and out of consciousness, resting comfortably with her head on my shoulder, stirring every now and then as I tried my best to wake her up. I was determined to get her back to the hotel for some much needed rest, not only for her own well-being, but before she further embarrassed me and herself. As I contemplated how to discreetly set about this task, the queen entered the room and sat beside us on the sofa.

"Stavros may be my first born son and heir to the throne..." she boasted, "but he has terrible taste in women."

The motherly tenderness I'd seen before was gone. The woman before me now was as cold as an iceberg.

"I beg your pardon?" I asked, raising a brow.

"This girl has no business being here," the queen stated. "And certainly no business rubbing elbows with a future king."

"That *girl* happens to be my best friend," I answered, archly.

The queen smiled.

"Like you, I'm fiercely protective of the people I love. *Especially,* my children...what is the nature of your relationship with my son?"

Tiffany growled, turned on her side, and snored loudly. I moved her head to the side to keep her from choking.

"Andrasi is my friend and employer," I answered defensively.

"But he's in love with you."

"Not possible. I hardly know him."

"We don't leap from person to person like Americans. In Capa, dating is a pathway to marriage and you're the first woman my son has ever brought home to us. As you may well already know, you bear an uncanny resemblance to *Magdalena.* Which I believe is the root of his fascination with you. Andrasi is an expert on the history of Capa."

"Who is Magdalena?" I asked.

The queen sighed.

"*Magdalena* was a Capa Queen of Moorish and Spanish blood…a relative of the ruling invader, and a woman of nobility. She was bartered to the King of Capa in 1495, after he overthrew Moorish invaders and recaptured the kingdom. We negotiated a truce, arranging a marriage between Magdalena and the son of the King. From that day forward, all future kings have been arranged in marriage to foreign women of nobility in order to establish peace with the rulers of other nations. Magdalena married the King's son, Agamemnon, but fell in love with Macurio, his younger brother. Macurio eventually poisoned his older brother, taking his wife and assuming the throne. As a result of his actions, the people threatened to overthrow Macurio but Agamemnon died. Even today, many argue that we are not a true lineage of Capa's ancient monarchy. Which of course, is rubbish. We are all of the same blood. My son is drawn to you because you remind him of Magdalena. You bear an uncanny resemblance to a woman whose ascent to the throne led to civil war and destruction."

"Regardless of how I look, I am not Magdalena and I would never do anything to hurt Andrasi."

The Queen removed a vial from her pocket, opened it, and waved it under Tiffany's nose. She awoke with a loud snort, blinking her eyes as she came to.

"Gawd, where am I?" she drooled.

"We're in Capa," I answered, dryly. "We're going back to the hotel."

I left Tiffany in the Queen's care, who despite her haughty attitude was surprisingly nurturing. I found Andrasi at the after-party with his brother Giovanni and his sister Agnes as they stood around the fireplace, recounting old times. I tapped him on the shoulder. He turned, his eyes lighting up at the sight of my face. Was his mother right? Was he really drawn to me because of my resemblance to Magdalena? It would be foolish to believe a woman who would say or do anything to control her son's life.

"I'm leaving," I said, trying not to appear upset.

"Is something wrong?" He looked concerned.

"Tiffany's not feeling well. I'm taking her back to the hotel. I need to call a cab."

"Don't be foolish, Selena. I will arrange for Harold to drive her back to the hotel, personally."

"I would appreciate it."

Andrasi summoned a waiter and gave him instructions for getting Tiffany back to the suite.

After arrangements had been made and Tiffany had been escorted safely to a waiting limo, Andrasi led me outside to the veranda where I was grateful to have a moment alone. I considered telling him what his mother said, but found it a difficult subject to broach. My best bet was to ignore his cackling witch of a mother and enjoy the rest of the evening with Andrasi, if at all possible.

"Thank heavens it's finally over!" I said, as we stood on the veranda, looking over the Queen's Garden.

"I felt like an idiot in there."

"You were fine," Andrasi assured me. "My father likes you."

"But your mother hates me."

"My mother hardly knows you."

"I'm a woman. I can tell by her disapproving glare. Not that it matters. I'll probably never see her again, anyway."

"What makes you say that?"

"I'm only here for two weeks, remember?"

"Hopefully, I can convince you to stay a while longer."

After the night I endured, staying in Capa any longer than needed was hardly an option.

"It doesn't work like that."

"How so?"

He looked disappointed. Was Andrasi really this clueless?

"I'm not royalty. I have a job and responsibilities at home. I can't do whatever I want without it affecting other people."

Andrasi took my hand within his and gazed into my eyes, his touch sending a jolt of electricity between my thighs.

"Then you admit you want me?"

His gaze was intense and mesmerizing…

"That's not what I said."

"Why deny it? I'll openly confess to anyone who asks. I enjoy every moment I spend with you. If I can't convince you to stay, then I hope you will allow me to spend as much time with you as I can before you leave."

I took a deep breath.

"We hardly know each other." My voice was barely a whisper—who was I trying to convince? Andrasi or myself?

"We know everything we need to know about each other for now. My hope, is to get to know you more intimately later."

The heat in his eyes intensified.

I withdrew my hand, removed the earrings from my ears and slapped them into the palm of his hands. Andrasi gave me a confused look.

"That's a little presumptuous of you, don't you think? I don't care who you are. I'm not your damned concubine, nor do I intend to be."

Before I could storm off, Andrasi grabbed my arm. Then he drew me close… his breath a whisper from my ear.

"Is that what it means to become intimate in your country? If I wanted sex, I would ask for it."

"Is that all it takes?" I asked, lifting my chin.

"Usually."

He leaned back, smiling smugly as he folded h his arms behind his head as he stretched.

"Besides…I don't seem to recall any of your objections the other night."

"How dare you hold that against me? I was vulnerable and distraught," I stammered.

"And yet, I did not take advantage of you. Not only that, I introduced you to my parents, who happen to be the King and Queen of Capa Isles. If that doesn't speak to my intentions, then there is no getting through to you."

"And what exactly are your intentions?" I asked, lifting my chin. "Because I can't seem to make them out. Within days of meeting you, you were already lavishing me with expensive clothes, jewels, and dinner with the royals—and I don't know why."

"When it comes to love, your culture is subtle. American couples take months or years to decide if they want to spend the rest of their lives together. That's not the way it works in Capa."

"What do you mean?"

Andrasi smacked a hand across his forehead.

"Are you always this dense?"

I rolled my eyes.

"Are you implying that you want to spend the rest of your life with me?"

"I'm not implying that I want to spend the rest of my life with you…I'm telling you *outright*," Andrasi answered.

"You're crazy," I said, scanning his face. *Was he serious?*

A servant appeared on the veranda with champagne. Andrasi took two glasses from the tray and handed one to me. As I imbibed the drink, I thought about the irony of getting jilted on my wedding day, only to have a man, a prince no less, proclaim his desire to spend the rest of his life with me days later. Our eyes met and the both of us suddenly laughed.

"That is quite possibly one of the worst lines I have ever heard."

"Well… I do try."

I wiped imaginary sweat from my forehead and sighed with relief. "Thanks for letting me off the hook. You had me going there for a second," I said, sighing in relief.

"It was worth it just to watch you squirm."

"What a scoundrel…" I grumbled, mockingly.

"Why is it so hard to believe that a man can fall head over heels for you?"

He took my empty glass away and signaled for another.

"Do American women believe in love at first sight?"

"Only the stupid ones."

He gave me a second glass of champagne. I drained it in one gulp. It was rare for me to drink so much, but it allowed me to focus on something other than Andrasi.

"Are you always this cynical?"

"Given the circumstances, can you blame me?"

Andrasi grabbed the rest of the champagne, loosened his tie, and drank directly from the bottle.

"Fair enough," he said, after a lengthy gulp. "What can I do to change your mind?"

I shrugged. "Nothing."

"I'm afraid to ask why." He looked disappointed.

Suddenly he was passing the champagne bottle. I took a swig then wiped the drizzle from my mouth with the back of my hand as we walked across the moonlit veranda.

"Nothing personal. I just don't happen to believe in love or that soul mate nonsense anymore."

"I'm crushed."

"You shouldn't be. I'm not cutting myself off."

"Does cutting yourself off emotionally count?"

"That's unfair," I exclaimed.

"Unfair to whom? The unlucky soul who finds himself attached to a jaded woman?"

"Now you're hitting below the belt."

I suddenly felt hot. I wasn't sure if it was Andrasi's interrogation or if the alcohol had taken affect. He took my hand.

"Let's take a walk."

The night was warm, perfect for a turn around the queen's lush green gardens. I left the empty champagne bottle on a patio table and followed Andrasi into the moonlit brush. From the Veranda, I saw a pristine waterfall cascading into a fountain surrounded by blooming moon flowers. The constellations were on full display in the sky. It was the perfect setting for an old world romance at an ancient medieval castle.

We strolled down a cobbled path to a field of green hedges and rosebushes sculpted into a labyrinth of mazes, walking silently until we were lost in the rich green shrubbery and each other. Ever so often a rose would appear, adding a burst of color to each bush. I watched them carefully, attempting to remember how to get back to the castle in vain.

"So…how lost are we?" I asked, staring up at the stars as if they would lead the way back.

"Lost? I know this maze like the back of my hand. My brothers and I played here as kids."

"Are you close to your brothers?"

"Used to be."

"What happened?"

Andrasi shrugged.

"Giovanni lives his life and Stavros is a reckless, irresponsible, womanizer."

"But he's the crown prince…" I said, surprised by Andrasi's tone.

"I don't give a damn. As the first born son it's his birthright. But I don't think he wants it."

"And you do?"

Andrasi smiled.

"I enjoy my freedom. I come and go as I please. I'm free to love and marry the woman of my choosing, while Stavros is forced to follow tradition and live the life of a royal. It's made him callous and miserable. But he is my brother and I love him dearly."

"What about your sister?"

"She's everything a sister should be and more. And that includes being a pain in the butt."

"That's high praise coming from you."

"She deserves nothing less. Do you have brothers or sisters?"

"I'm an only child."

"I figured as much. You have a lonely quality about you."

Andrasi took my hand and led me to a rose covered gazebo in the middle of a clearing. We brushed the flowers and a thick covering of ivy aside and entered. With only the moonlight streaming into the dark interior through an opening in the roof for light, I followed Andrasi to a chaise lounge and sat beside him. A gentle breeze pushed a wooden swing to and fro in the night.

"I'm not lonely," I said.

"Not anymore," Andrasi answered, gently caressing my arms.

He opened the interior of his suit jacket, revealing a bottle of champagne.

"I swiped it from a table on our way out."

"That's pretty slick," I said, admiring his cat-burglar-like skills.

Andrasi popped the cork and took a swig.

"I slipped it in my pants. My brothers and I used to steal liquor and drink it out here in the gazebo."

"Weren't you a bunch of naughty kids!"

"Naughty, bored, whatever you want to call it."

He passed the bottle to me. I took lengthy gulp and tried not to belch.

"You're the first woman I've ever brought to Queen's Garden."

"Why me?" I asked, surprised by the revelation.

Andrasi signed. "Most women want to see the castle, the royal crown and jewels, or meet the king and queen. You're not like that."

"While I'm enjoying my walk in the Queen's Garden and spending time with you in the gazebo, your family's history is fascinating to me."

I especially wanted to know more about Andrasi's connection to Magdalena.

"That's different. Most women don't want to feel like a princess, they want to be a princess. Their only interest in San Bianca Castle is materialistic."

"So they're gold-diggers? Can you blame them? Little girls are showered with pink dresses and gifts and told they're a princess at birth. We're bred to seek our prince or knight in shining armor."

"Being a prince or a princess isn't all it's cracked up to be."

He pushed me against the chaise and pressed his muscular physique onto mine.

"Life isn't all it's cracked up to be," I answered, pretending to be unfazed by the proximity of his manliness.

With the moonlight striking his face, Andrasi was more than handsome. He was luminous… beautiful in a way that filled me with both envy and desire. I'd seen the same look reflecting back at me from his eyes.

I took a final sip of champagne. I was starting to feel tipsy. We lay facing each other on the chaise, our legs coiled together as we finished the last of the champagne. I rubbed a hand across Andrasi's massive chest. I loved the feel of his warm, muscular flesh beneath my palms. He furrowed his dark eyebrows together. *Are you sure?* Though he dare not ask, for fear I might answer.

But I was more than sure. I was ready. I was ready to move forward with my life, ready to begin anew. I closed my eyes and kissed him gently, my tongue delving into his mouth. This was all the confirmation he needed. With Marvin it was different. He'd made it clear that making love to me was an obligation… confirmation in his mind that we were a couple. It was a love forged out of loyalty until the day he cheated on me, severing the final strand that bound us together.

With Andrasi, the tension emanating between us burbled below the surface, threatening to erupt like a volcano, drowning us both in orgasmic lava and white hot heat. So intense was our fiery passion, that he undressed me, slowly unzipping the back of my dress as his lips traced the curve of my neck, the tremors cooling me down as his red-hot touch warmed me up again. He drew the pins from my hair, releasing it, so that my tousled hair fell over my shoulders.

"You're so beautiful," Andrasi said, coiling his fingers in my hair. "I've wanted this from the moment I laid eyes on you."

He drew me to me his lap so that I straddled him. He was fully clothed, still in his suit as I sat facing him, my legs over his hips.

"Undress me," Andrasi whispered.

His breathing was so ragged his entire body vibrated with every breath.

I quietly removed his tie and dropped it on top of my heap of discarded clothes. Then I slowly unbuttoned his shirt, popping the buttons one by one, my hands roaming over the swell of his chest, down his abdomen, to his thick leather belt. I unbuckled it, ripped it through the loops in one motion, cracking the air as I tossed it on the grass. Then I peeled his shirt off and flung it over my shoulder. I cradled his head in my arms as he buried his face between breasts and suckled my nipples, his powerful hands encompassing them as he moved them in a circular motion.

"Unbutton my pants," Andrasi breathed, guiding my hand to his lap.

I swiftly unbuckled his pants and reached into the tent of what had become of his underwear.

He groaned, tensing until his entire body convulsed with desire. His hands tightened around my waist, as he slid out of his pants, lifted my dress, and in one powerful thrust…our molten hot bodies became one.

Chapter Five

The moonlight streaming into the gazebo illuminated Andrasi's face in the darkness. With only a dense covering of ivy clinging to the gazebo to conceal us from prying eyes, I felt protected as he drew me into the nook of his muscular arms and covered me with his flesh. I rested with my head on his perspired chest and played with his navel as he traced a hand along my shoulder. Was it possible to fall for someone this soon? And what about his mother? She made it clear that a commoner like me wasn't good enough for her royal son. The last thing I needed in my life was more rejection, especially from her.

"So where do we go from here?" Andrasi asked, brushing my tousled hair away from my face. He kissed the top of my head.

"Back to the hotel for round two," I smiled.

His dark features hardened. "I'm serious, Selena."

"So am I…do we have to define what we have? We're' enjoying each other. That's it."

I'm just having some fun, I quietly reminded myself. I rolled out of his arms and gathered my clothes.

"*That's it*?" he repeated.

"Only if you want it to be."

I continued dressing.

"Why are you being so difficult?"

Because you're a royal and your mother hates me! I told her I wanted nothing from her son or her family, and I was bound to keep my word.

Andrasi's movements were jerky as he snapped his clothes from the ground and proceeded to get dressed. I searched the grass for my hair pins, finding them one by one. As I stopped to fix my hair, Andrasi sidled up to me from behind and nuzzled my neck. I couldn't resist him. I relaxed into his embrace, his touch making me shudder from head to toe.

"I didn't mean to pressure you. I'm sorry," he whispered into my ear, his voice quivering with emotion.

"I'm not sure I forgive you," I pouted. "You'll have to do something to make it up to me later," I teased.

He smiled, his eyes overflowing with relief.

We took a short cut through the maze to get back to the San Bianca Castle, where Andrasi bade his siblings and parents goodbye. At least… everyone but Stavros, who was nowhere to be found.

"Where is he?" I asked, unable to hide my curiosity and concern.

"Somewhere brooding is my guess," Andrasi answered, casually.

"Would your parents consider letting him chart his own path someday? The traditions the royal family have placed on Stavros have made him so unhappy."

I felt genuinely sorry for the man.

"Absolutely not. It is what it is, Selena. He knew what he was getting into when he accepted the crown."

We climbed into the Maybach. Harold was already back from his trip to the hotel, where Tiffany was delivered safe and sound.

"How is she?" I asked, after we were firmly seated in the car.

"She's awake and alert. Someone is there to watch over her. She'll be *fine*."

He rolled his eyes. I caught a glimpse of his disgruntled face in the rearview mirror as the partition closed between us. The smell of pine air freshener and cleaning solution lingered in the air. I started to roll the window down, when it occurred to me that Tiffany had thrown up in Andrasi's car, leaving Harold to clean the mess, if the smudge of vomit on the passenger side door was any indication. I sighed. Andrasi kissed the back of my hand and pulled me close. Harold had taken a less scenic route back to the hotel, driving through busy city streets that reminded me of home.

Soon we were on the elevator back at the hotel. When we reached our floor, Andrasi swept me off of my feet and carried me upstairs to the master bedroom.

"I had a wonderful time tonight," Andrasi said, gently placing me on the bed. He kneeled before me, taking my heels off, his fingers playfully caressing my legs.

"So did I…" I whispered, hesitantly.

"But?" He furrowed his brows, his dark hypnotic eyes transfixed on my face.

"…I'd like to apologize for my friend's behavior."

"Why? She's an adult. You're not responsible for her actions. What Tiffany did bears no reflection on you."

"But I invited her to Capa and invited her to the party…she also mortified and upset the Queen, I'm sure. I was so embarrassed."

"Embarrassed by what?" he scoffed. "The only opinion you need to worry about is mine."

He pulled my dress over my head in one swoop and dropped it on the floor.

"Is that so?" I asked, surprised by his arrogant tone.

Andrasi ripped his shirt off revealing his bare chest. My body flushed at the sight of his impressive physique.

"You can do no wrong in my eyes, so what does it matter?" he answered confidently.

"It matters to your mother," I finally admitted.

"Why do you care about what my mother thinks? She's not the one who has to sleep with you at night."

"Neither do you."

"I don't have to, I *want* to," he said, crawling into bed and climbing over me.

I wrapped my arms around his neck and ran my fingers through the prickly hair on the nape of his neck. Andrasi's lips brushed gently across mine then trailed along the side of my neck to my shoulder, then back to my chest, where he nibbled my exposed nipples. I mentally smiled at the idea that an uptight, recently dumped librarian could ever be involved in a whirlwind romance…making passionate love to a handsome prince on a beautiful Mediterranean island. I was living out fantasies women would only dared to dream about. I felt uninhibited, infatuated, and completely under Andrasi's spell. I wanted to give myself to him completely, feel him inside of me. He groaned as his lips met mine, passionately, this time, his tongue delving into the warmth of my mouth as his hands roamed the swell of my breasts. I trailed kisses all over his chest and face, stopping at his ear, to suck the lobe. He removed his pants, grunting as he tossed them over his shoulder, his hardened sex tensing and lengthening with excitement against my inner thigh as my legs parted to meet him. I felt a pin-prick of pain, followed by intense pleasure.

After our session of unbridled love-making, I lay in Andrasi's arms, fast asleep as he snored softly in my ear. But it was a sound, a cry in the middle of the night that awakened us. It sounded, not quite like a woman, but not like a man either. I wasn't even sure it was human.

"What is that?" I said, waking from a deep sleep. Alarmed, I shook Andrasi's arm. He sat up, and looked over the railing into the living room, which was still dark.

"It's nothing, go back to sleep," he groaned, drawing me back into the nook of his arms. Andrasi tried locking his arms around me but I pushed him aside and tossed the covers back.

I heard the voice again and bolted upright.

"I'm serious, Andrasi. Something is wrong with Tiffany."

He smacked his lips. "I'm positive-honey… there's nothing wrong with your friend."

"Are you sure?"

He responded by tugging my elbow until I crawled back into position, resting in the nook of his arms. Finally, the voice screamed again. I climbed out of bed and marched down the stairs, ignoring Andrasi's impatient groan. I followed the sound of the screaming, which sounded more and more like moaning as I neared Tiffany's room and banged on the door. After some stumbling and the sound of items being knocked over, she finally opened the door stark naked, her mood as calm as the sea.

"Are you okay? I heard you scream…" I panted, anxious about the commotion. I averted my eyes at first, then peeked over her shoulder and peered into the room. To my surprise, Tiffany wasn't alone. Stavros was in her bed. He had been blindfolded and was tied to the headboard with pantyhose.

"Anything else?" she asked, quirking an eyebrow.

I shook my head and backed away. With the crack of the black leather belt in her hand, Tiffany smirked then closed the door as Stavros screamed out again. I turned the lights back off and went upstairs.

"Is everything okay?" Andrasi queried, as I climbed back in bed.

"Sometimes in life, there are things you wish you could un-see... this is one of them," I droned, drawing the covers over my head.

Chapter Six

"Morning, Sunshine," Tiffany said, helping herself to a piece of toast as she sat at the dining room table.

Daniella poured enough orange juice and glasses of water to accommodate four guests. It was safe to assume that Stavros was still in the suite. But where was Andrasi? I sat at the table and helped myself to a bagel and two slices of bacon.

"A messenger from the royal family was here this morning. You are hereby summoned to San Bianca Castle," said Daniella excitedly. "They would like you to begin work on the library next week."

I perked up. "Wonderful," I exclaimed. "I was hoping to have a look at the library last night, but didn't get the chance," *...thanks to Tiffany,* I thought.

"It's like a museum honey, that area of the castle is probably closed. In fact, I believe it's been closed for some time."

"Are you working for the royal family?" Tiffany asked. "That queen was a real bitch."

I heard an intake of breath. Daniella stopped dead in her tracks to glare at Tiffany before going back into the kitchen.

I shushed her.

"You can't talk like that," I gasped. "You'll get arrested!"

"I can talk however I want," Tiffany said. "Queen or not, she can kiss my natural ass. She was just plain rude to you and everyone else."

"And yet, she nurtured you back to consciousness after you blacked out last night. She can't be *that* bad."

"Bad enough. She's making Stavros miserable," Tiffany complained.

The elevator doors opened. Stavros, Andrasi, and six secret service agents walked in behind them. Andrasi directed the men to wait in the foyer and living room while he ate, then gestured for Daniella to serve them drinks.

"Hey babe, want some breakfast?" Tiffany asked.

"Sure," Stavros answered, smiling as he walked to the table with red welts on his arms.

Tiffany rolled her eyes. "I wasn't talking to you," she scoffed. "I was talking to your security guards."

He sat beside her and grabbed a glass of orange juice. They acted like an old married couple.

"Honey, they're secret service agents," Stavros replied. He bit into a piece of toast.

After breakfast we went to the beach where the paparazzi took photos of us from the rooftop of a nearby hotel, despite the fact that we were sunbathing on a private beach. I wondered if news of my relationship with Andrasi had reached newspapers, and family and friends back home. *Marvin, eat your heart out!* Andrasi and Stavros drank wine, ate strawberry croquettes, and an olive and walnut salad, while Tiffany and I deftly avoided the delicious high calorie snacks.

We eventually separated from the couple for lunch, with me and Andrasi taking a trip to the countryside to see the medieval cross I'd been fascinated with. Turns out, the cross was also a lighthouse overlooking the olive orchards with a breathtaking view of the sparkling blue-green sea surrounding Capa. From the top, we could see Mount Stromboli, an active volcano on an island off the shores of Sicily. Daniella packed our meal into a picnic basket. We ate a romantic dinner in the kitchen of the lighthouse and slept on an uncomfortable cot on the top floor, where we also made love. The following day we toured ancient landmarks and cave dwellings where we examined the cave writings of pre-civilization Capa. Then sailed on Andrasi's yacht to the Aeolian Islands where we hiked on Lipari, the next day. We made love in the ship's cramped cabin on the way home, which left my muscles so sore that we went to the boutique afterwards for a massage.

The following day we walked through olive orchards, and later, expansive grape vineyards... which was a first for me. Capa Isles had a multi-billion dollar wine and olive oil export, a company of which, Andrasi was the CEO. We made love immediately, and fervently, in his office after the tour. It occurred to me then that I still ended up on my honeymoon, just with the wrong man. Or was he the right man all along? *Was this destiny?* It wasn't long before the weekend was over and with less than a week left in Capa, I wondered if I would ever see him again. We spent the next few days much the same. Sightseeing, riding a yacht, and making love.

By request, Harold drove me to San Bianca Castle first thing, early Wednesday morning. Andrasi had already left for the day on a short business trip. It was our first time apart in over a week and I already missed him. Upon arrival at the king and queen's estate, I was greeted by a staff person who took me to an office on the second floor of the castle to meet the curator, Jacoby Hills, a British scholar specializing in ancient Greek and Mediterranean culture.

"Pleasure to meet you, Miss Capshaw," he said, in an aloof British accent that sounded welcoming at the same time. "I trust you've been briefed."

"Unfortunately, I have not," I said, adopting the same aloof professional demeanor I used in meetings with city officials at work. I wore a suit jacket, button-down shirt, slacks, and my hair in a bun.

"The royal library was maintained by household staff, but unfortunately wasn't properly organized. Our objective is to update the library using an American cataloguing system."

There were shelves upon shelves of burgundy colored leather-bound books, all of them in impeccable shape, despite their age. According to Jacoby, some of the books were well over a century or two old. While the leather-bound covers were still intact, the pages had turned yellow. I used a PowerPoint presentation to discuss appropriate room temperature and other strategies for preserving the pages of old books. The books were also written in a foreign language, so I couldn't determine the genre, much less how to catalogue them. Fortunately, Jacoby was a scholar and could translate ancient Greek and Latin text.

After several hours of work, drafting a blueprint for the layout of the books with Jacoby, I left the library in search of the lavatory. I roamed the corridors of the massive castle, hoping to find a butler or maid who could point me in the right direction, but saw no one, not even a guard. Jacoby directed me to the lavatory, but I somehow managed to miss it. I opened several doors, some of them leading to a closet, office, or stairway leading out of the castle. I was grateful when I heard voices filtering out of a nearby parlor room into the corridor. One of them, was the unmistakable voice of the queen, the other, was Andrasi. I walked down the hall towards the voices, but stopped shy of the door before entering.

"It's your fault, Andrasi. You invited that tramp into our lives and you're responsible for getting rid of her."

"I've grown tired of her too, but I'm a man of my word. I can't ask her to leave."

"She's ruining our lives as we speak," the queen sneered. "I can't believe this is happening…" her voice quivered with emotion.

"Fine, mother," Andrasi groaned. "I'll make arrangements to have her placed on the next flight to the United States. Happy now?"

The sound of Andrasi's voice grew faint as I moved down the hall as fast as my feet could carry me, tears stinging my eyes. I thought Andrasi actually liked me but he was bad as Marvin…no, *worse*. He took advantage of me after I had been left at the altar and had already been in considerable pain. *Hadn't I been through enough?* Andrasi used me, and was planning to dump me on the next plane back to the States at the behest of his wicked mother. But I wasn't about to sit around and wait for Andrasi to dump me. I stopped and leaned against the wall for support, heaving as tears flowed from my eyes. I was sick of betrayal. He didn't have to kick me out. I would leave on my own volition.

I composed myself as much as I could, then called Harold and told him I was ready to go. He arrived in record time to my relief, and drove me back to the suite. I asked him to wait while I crammed my clothes into my luggage without folding them, managing to pack my belongings in under twenty minutes.

"Take me to the airport please," I said.

Harold hauled my suitcases to the car and placed them in the trunk.

"I'll call the Prigkipas to let him know where we're going."

"I'd prefer if you didn't do that," I answered, tersely.

"I'm not allowed to—" Harold started.

I gave him a pleading look, my eyes filled with tears. "Please, I'm begging you…if you can't take me, direct me to someone who can. I have an emergency back home, I will contact Andrasi as soon as I'm back in the States," I lied.

"I could lose my job…" Harold nervously, replied.

I sighed. I wasn't trying to ruin the man's life. But why would he lose his job when Andrasi wanted me gone anyway? If anything, he'll probably get a bonus.

"Andrasi has been made aware of my emergency. He'll understand," I pleaded. "Please, get me to the airport," I cried.

With a sigh, Harold climbed into the driver's seat. An hour later we were at the airport, where I wiped used all of savings to buy a ticket home. I bade Harold goodbye, wishing I had the nerve to ask him to lie about my whereabouts. My heart raced as I waited to board the plane. It would take Andrasi an hour to get to the airport. There was still time to escape with *some* of my dignity left intact. Finally, the door to the cabin opened and the passengers were escorted inside one by one. Soon, the plane took off and no Andrasi. Deep inside, I hoped he would come and beg me to stay, but he never arrived.

Tiffany was so engrossed in her relationship with Stavros that she hardly noticed I was gone. But I sent a text message anyway, telling her I had gone back home. I stared out of my window at the clouds and cried, most of the way home. Was I in love with Andrasi? No. That was impossible. It was too soon. *But why did my heart ache so?*

Chapter Seven

It was a week after arriving back home when the tears finally stopped and life went back to normal. Upon my return, I went to lunch with my parents as promised, but lied about my Mediterranean adventure and the reason why I returned three days early. I used an extra week of vacation to sort through my emotions before going back to work. It didn't help when I passed a tabloid at a newspaper stand bearing a picture of Andrasi with an awkward picture of me in a red dress and a caption that read, *"IT'S OVER! Prince dumps American, moves on to Miss Universe."* I remembered the hairstylist at the Royal Blue Boutique's words... *"You get used to the lifestyle he provides then one day it goes away when he tires of you. Then you have to get used to being normal again...."*

I reorganized my apartment, painted my bedroom, and purchased new pillows for my couch. The fluffy lacy kind, that elderly women buy.

It was a few weeks later when I stood in living room in my nightgown, prepared to devour a pint of peanut butter ice cream and oatmeal cookies when the phone rang. I immediately recognized the voice on the other end of the line, and instantly regretted answering.

"I need to see you," Marvin pleaded, urgency in his voice.

"I'm busy," I answered tersely.

"Yes, I know…but it's important. Please, for old time's sake, just hear me out."

"What is this about?" I asked, somewhat curious, despite not wanting to see his lying face again.

"Us."

I sat the ice cream on the counter.

"There is no *us*. You saw to that, remember?"

"You might change your mind when you hear what I have to say. We were…" he paused, "we were swindled."

I sighed, my curiosity was piqued. Marvin could tell me whatever he wanted, I would never allow him into my heart again.

"Fine. Be here in fifteen minutes. You have five minutes to say what you have to say then you must leave."

After the situation with Andrasi, I wasn't in a forgiving mood.

Ten minutes later I heard a knock on the door. I opened it, and Marvin stumbled inside. His face was unshaven, his clothes disheveled, and he smelled of liquor.

"What on earth is wrong with you, coming here in this state?"

His eyes were full of tears. He grabbed me and forcefully pulled me into his arms. "I missed you so much," Marvin cried, burying his face into my shoulder.

"You have four minutes," I coldly reminded him.

He walked over to the sofa and sat down. I carried my ice cream with me, eating it straight out of the carton with a spoon.

"I saw the pictures," he mumbled. "It was all over the tabloids."

"Ah huh…"

I crumbled oatmeal cookies into the carton of ice cream and shoveled another teaspoon into my mouth.

"Andrasi was my friend. I invited him to our wedding."

I lifted a brow. "Your point?"

"He's trying to ruin my life."

I wasn't interested in listening to Marvin's unfolding melodrama.

"What does that have to do with me?"

"He manipulated me into leaving you so he could have you for himself."

"Rubbish. I didn't even meet the man until you dumped me on our wedding day."

"Did you sleep with him?"

"Yes…" I answered blithely.

Marvin broke down, sobbing into the palm of his hands.

The glacier residing in my heart started to melt.

"Why are you crying?" I asked. "You wanted your cheerleader and you got her. I'm not standing in your way and neither is Andrasi. Go. Be happy. I'm not mad at you anymore. I've moved on with my life."

"Don't you see? It was a setup. Candace suddenly appeared a week before our wedding, after three long years. She begged me to take her back. After I left you on our wedding day for her, Candace dumped me. Realizing I made a mistake, I looked for you. We should have gotten married. I wanted you back. I even flew to Capa but was turned away by their immigration office at the airport. Next thing you know, I see you in the tabloids with Andrasi. Then it clicked. It finally clicked when stocks for CreeGee Software plummeted. I immediately dumped my shares, which were controlling shares of the company. Then someone purchased them within minutes and took a controlling share of the company. I learned, it was Capa Industries. Andrasi is one of the most ruthless businessmen I know. He manipulated the stock market by purchasing a large quantity of shares over a period of time then strategically dumped them on our wedding day to distract me."

My spoon was hanging out of my mouth by the time he finished.

"Why would he do this? It doesn't make sense…and what does that have to do with me?" Especially considering that Andrasi never wanted me in the first place.

"He wanted you. I saw it in his eyes…this look of appreciation, lust, and greed."

"You're not only out of your mind, but your four minutes are up. Please leave."

"He hired a private investigator to look into my past. That's how he found out about Candace. He paid her to separate us so he could have you for himself."

"That's absurd."

I rose from my seat on the sofa and opened the door.

Marvin dropped to his knees and threw himself at my feet, arms reaching up as he clung to my waist.

"Blame Andrasi all you want. In the end, you made the choice to dump me for another woman on our wedding day."

"Because he suggested it was the right thing to do."

"Serves you right for being weak-minded. We're done, Marvin. We can never go back to what we were. Now please leave. It's over."

Marvin picked himself up and strode out the door. "You're the best thing that ever happened to me. I love you. I'll never give up on you, Selena."

And with those final words, I closed the door behind him. I listened near the door until the sound of his feet on the stairs faded away, then dropped to my knees and sobbed. I knew the moment he walked through my door, that I was no longer in love with him. My adrenaline no longer raced, my stomach didn't flip, or feel like it was full of butterflies. How did everything go so wrong?

The next day I planted vegetables and flowers in my potted vegetable garden and lounged on my patio wearing a straw hat and glamorous designer sunglasses. I fell asleep in the warm sunshine, but not long after, was awakened by my ringing cell phone. To my surprise, it was Marvin again.

"Care to join me for dinner tonight?" he asked. "They're serving your favorite dish at LaTrolle Pasta."

"Thanks but no thanks," I answered. "I'm not in the mood." I was lovesick, but not for him.

"I owe you an apology and I'd prefer to do it in person," he said.

"An apology for what?" I asked.

"Last night, and for ruining our wedding."

It was going to take more than an apology to win me over. Not romantically, but at least to forgive him as a human being. It was obvious that the both of us needed closure.

"Fine. We'll have dinner. But that's it."

"Thank you, Selena. I won't disappoint you."

"Too late for that," I answered, hanging up.

We met for dinner and I ate lasagna, chicken parmigiana and Manicotti. A three-dish meal." I picked at the food with my fork as Marvin poured his heart out.

"It's so good to see your face," he said. "I don't care about the bad business deal with Andrasi or whatever you did with him in Capa. I don't care. I want you back. It's my fault. I can't blame you for what you did."

"What I did?" I repeated, incredulous.

"I want you back," Marvin said, reaching across the table.

That's not going to happen," I answered, pulling my hand away.

"Why? Why won't you take me back?" he pleaded.

"Because I'm not in love with you anymore."

"You don't mean that. You just don't fall out of love with people overnight."

"You hurt me, Marvin. You hurt me deeply, and I can't get over that. I know where I stand with you and I will never forget it."

"*I'm sorry*. If I could do anything to take your pain away, I would."

"Don't' flatter yourself. I'm not hurt anymore."

"Then at least let me be your friend again," he said.

"Fine. I'm open to being friends, but that's it."

He sighed, his eyes overflowing with relief.

"Can we end the tension between us, now?"

"Maybe," I smiled.

"Are you done mentally beating my ass for breaking up with you on our wedding day?"

"I'll have to think about it…" I grinned, pondering.

I finished my pasta and pushed the plate to the center of the table.

"That really hit the spot," I grinned.

"I bet it did. You're eating more than you used to. You used to nibble but now you're eating an entire three course meal. You were eating a pint of ice cream right out of the carton last time I saw you. It really drove home how much I hurt you. I know how careful you are about your diet. Don't turn to food like I did when I was depressed," he said, reminding me of when he was a 350lb man.

It didn't take long for Marvin and me to get back on good terms, even though I still refused to take him back. It was like we reverted back to the relationship we had before we first started dating. He seemed to have a newfound appreciation for me. Despite this, I realized I could never take him back. After the Candace debacle, Marvin had shown me would dump me again if the right woman came along.

I went back to work a few days after our dinner date, and still no sign of Tiffany. I was starting to worry. I eventually received a call from her assuring me that she would return from Capa soon, and asked to use another two week's vacation. I approved her time off and told her to tell Andrasi I no longer worked at the library if asked. She told me that she no longer sees him, and that she and Stavros have been hiding out. I found it ironic that Tiffany's relationship with Stavros lasted longer than my relationship with Andrasi.

She returned to work four weeks later. I asked what happened, but she refused to discuss it, only saying that she'd grown tired of Stavros and his clinginess, and that they had broken up. I was happy to have my friend back. I was certain now, that the princes were finally behind us. I was even starting to get over my all-too-brief, relationship with Andrasi…that is, until I went to the doctor.

Chapter Eight

"You're pregnant," Dr. McAndrews said. "Based on my calculations, you're about seven weeks along. Congratulations."

A wave of nausea made my stomach churn like I had the flu. "Are you sure?" I asked. "How is this possible?"

"Are you asking me to explain the birds and the bees?"

I shook my head. "I'm stunned."

"It's wonderful news. You should be thankful."

I felt like slapping the doctor across his chubby face.

Thankful for what? Thankful to be pregnant by a man who wants nothing to do with me? A prince, whose royal family could see my child as some sort of threat? A child whose paternal grandmother hates my guts? A child who would be subjected to the paparazzi and a hostile public, who might condemn him for being born out of wedlock? I walked home from the doctor's office weighing my options. I could have an abortion and spare myself and the child a life of misery. Or I could tell no one about the child's parentage and raise him or her on my own. I took a detour into the local supermarket and purchased a carton of peanut butter ice cream, watermelon, and oatmeal cookies. The cashier gave me a funny look as I paid for my groceries. If it was hard to get over Andrasi before, it would be even harder now, knowing the child we created was nestled inside of me.

I fell asleep that night with tears in my eyes. Tears of joy? Sadness? I wanted to blame Marvin, but couldn't. *How could I be so stupid?*

I hid the pregnancy from my family and friends for as long as I could. I was three and a half months along when I finally sat them down, and revealed my secret. To my surprise, mother was ecstatic. My father on the other hand, refused to accept my reticent response, when he asked about the father. I managed to tell him the truth without revealing much. That I met the father in Capa and that I would never see him again. Thankfully, my parents stayed away from the tabloids. Still, I would have to keep the pregnancy under wraps in the event that some nosy tabloid journalist with lousy math skills put two and two together. I also kept Tiffany in the dark. If asked, I would allude, somehow, that Marvin was the father. Though in reality, it was impossible, as we had not been intimate for more than a month before the wedding.

Marvin and I spent time together occasionally, as friends, but slowly drifted apart when he realized I would never take him back. I kept him in the dark about the pregnancy. It was for the best.

As an expectant mother, I enjoyed the attention, eating whatever I wanted, the joy of buying cute maternity clothes. I also loved shopping for baby toys and supplies with my mother. It gave us the chance to bond all over again. She even agreed to babysit while I worked, as she was already retired and had more than enough free time on her hands. I had a strong support system… a network of friends and family who would help when the baby was born. I was already starting to show, and my breasts were already full at three and a half months. Some pregnant women, I'm told, are depressed…and some are happy. I was one of the happy ones, even without the child's father in our lives.

As I prepared the baby's room, adding a new set of toys and baby bottles, I heard a knock on the door. I looked out the window and saw a squad car and flashing police lights. I immediately opened the door.

"Miss Capshaw? I'm Detective Wilson, and this is FBI agent Martina Turner."

Both of the law enforcement officers flashed their badges. A man in a suit stood beside them. "I'm Bill Christenson, from ICE, the Federal Immigration and Customs Enforcement. May I come in?"

I moved aside, allowing the three officers to walk in. "Absolutely, how may I help you?"

"I'm afraid we will need to escort you to the police station for processing. You're being extradited."

"I beg your pardon? What do you mean, extradited? On what charges?"

"Kidnapping," the FBI agent said.

My legs nearly gave out.

"Is this some sort of prank? How could I be accused of kidnapping? Do you see any children around here?"

The immigration officer stuck his head into the baby's room.

"I see a room being prepared for an infant."

"Of course, I'm an expectant mother!"

I felt so weak my legs finally gave way. The officers caught me before I fell and led me to the sofa.

"You're being extradited to Capa Isles, where charges were filed against you."

"Are you insane? Why the hell would someone in Capa press charges against me? I want an attorney. I am an American citizen and I have rights! You can't just extradite me to some foreign country on a trumped up charge."

"The kidnapping charge violates international agreements with Capa. So Detective Wilson will book you. Because you crossed state lines, you also violated Federal laws. And of course, immigration laws, considering, the child is the citizen of another country."

"I don't understand..." I said. "We haven't established paternity. The child isn't even born yet."

"That's expected to be sorted out when you arrive in Capa. The United States has extradition treaties with many European countries. Capa is one of them. They guaranteed us immediate extradition upon request, and we grant them the same in return," Agent Turner said.

"This is un-American," I countered.

"Unfortunately, it is not," the immigration agent continued. "Your unborn child was conceived in Capa Isles, making the child a citizen of that country automatically per Capa immigration law. Citizens of Capa Isles must be born on Capa soil or file formal paperwork, if the child is to be born on foreign territory. Because this child is already a citizen of another country, proper paperwork and a visa is required before the child can enter the country."

"I am his mother. Children born in other countries to pregnant American women are automatically granted American citizenship."

"Unfortunately, your child is unborn, so the law does not apply. Capa Isles has already established citizenship. There is also a matter of the custodial dispute between you and the paternal parent."

"He's not the father," I exclaimed.

"We'll let the courts decide," Officer Wilson, said. "Now please come with us."

I finally stood, unwilling to fight any longer for fear of becoming so stressed, that I would end up having a miscarriage. I decided to sort things out in Capa. I would call my parents after arrival, and have them meet me in the country with an attorney. A team of immigration specialists packed my bags and dumped them into a waiting car. The baby's clothing and other belongings were also carried along. After processing at the local police station, I was taken directly to the airport, where my heart nearly stopped out of pure shock when I saw the silver, Bombardier BD-700 Global Express…Andrasi's luxury airplane.

"The prince offered his airplane to assure your safety during the long flight. The airplane has been equipped with the necessary medical equipment and medical staff if needed," Agent Turner said. A pair of handlers helped escort me up the stairs as I boarded the airplane. I was too anxious to feel angry. I hadn't seen the man in months. Would the longing in my eyes give my feelings away? Did he deserve my love? Of course not. He not only rejected me, but subjected me to a humiliating arrest. But how did he know about the baby? Only friends and family in my immediate circle knew about the pregnancy. *Did Tiffany open her big mouth?*

Soon, I was aboard the flight where I was escorted to one of the cabins and instructed to rest on the comfortable all white bed. I sighed with relief. No Andrasi yet. The agent said the prince allowed me to use his plane. She didn't say he would be on it.

"Can I help you with anything?" a tall, blonde-haired, male flight attendant asked.

"May I have a bowl of ice cream, with crumbled oatmeal cookies, please? Preferably oatmeal with cranberries?" I asked.

"Of course…the man answered. I'll see what we have available."

"Thank you," I answered.

As the flight attendant departed, another presence filled the room. I looked up to find Andrasi standing in the doorway. I couldn't get over the devastated look on his face when he saw me.

I put my hands on my hips. "What is the meaning of this?" I asked, getting straight to the point.

"You're carrying my child. He belongs in Capa with his family."

"You don't know anything about this baby, or my pregnancy. It's not yours."

"I know math, and that's enough. You're three and a half months along, which proves you're carrying my child."

"You have no right to tear me away from my family or my life. Let alone the right to have me arrested to get what you want."

"I did what I had to do to see you again."

"You lost that right months ago."

"What..." he said, pausing as he strode across the room towards me, "did I do to make you run off like that? What would make you stick a knife in a man's heart and twist it over and over again? Not only did you leave without warning, you tried to keep my child away from me," he ranted, the look in his dark eyes turning bitter and cold.

"I left because you wanted me to!" I spat, eyes swelling with tears. "I overheard you and your mother. She told you to get rid of me. You said you were tired of me anyway, and would stick me on the next flight moving to the States. Well, I did you both a favor and left on my own."

I raised my chin. Andrasi sat on the corner of the bed, his shoulders slumping forward.

"Is that what this is about? When I said, *I was tired of her anyway*, I wasn't talking about you. I was talking about your friend, Tiffany. My mother wanted her gone and for a good reason. You have no idea what she's done."

I stared at Andrasi, astounded. Suddenly, I was the one who felt like a fool.

"I'm afraid to ask…" I whispered.

"Stavros asked Tiffany to marry him, and she agreed. Of course, mother wouldn't stand for it, and demanded to have her deported. But he refused to give her up. My parents gave him a choice. Give her up, or renounce his throne. Stavros chose to renounce his throne and eloped. Or so we thought."

"Oh no…" I said, hand covering my mouth. "Then Giovanni the III is now the crown prince," I said.

Andrasi shook his head. "Unfortunately, I inherited the crown."

"How is that possible? You're third in line."

"Yes—but Giovanni lives a secret life. Well, an open secret, anyway. Giovanni prefers the company of men."

"Oh," was all I said. "And you accepted the crown? Congratulations to you and yours."

"And that includes my son or daughter, who will inherit the crown from me."

I shook my head. "I want no part of this royal business. Besides, isn't it true that your parents would arrange a marriage between you and a woman of nobility?"

"I already have a wife," Andrasi said, rubbing his palm over the swell of my belly. "The woman already carrying my child."

"We're not married," I countered.

"According to Capa law, we are."

I sat beside him. "I don't understand..." "In Capa, if a man impregnates a woman, they are considered legally married by law. This was established centuries ago to protect our women from vagabonds and louts. If a man is already married, and impregnates a second woman, he is considered legally married to both women and must divide his time and wealth between two homes. He is also jailed for his lascivious crimes. We have a very low to nonexistent out-of-wedlock birth rate in Capa. Infidelity is highly frowned upon."

"How did you know about the pregnancy?"

"Your mother confirmed it. I followed her into a baby store and casually asked who she was shopping for. She said her daughter is three and a half months pregnant. You told me you were an only child. I also noticed that you made frequent visits to the doctor and I was able to put two and two together."

My head was spinning.

"So you were following me."

"I wanted to know everything about you. Anything I could use against to get even with you for breaking my heart."

Suddenly, Marvin's warning about Andrasi started to ring true. The queen worried that I was a reincarnation of Magdalena, out to destroy her family. I wasn't Magdalena. Andrasi *was* Macurio.

"I told you once, that our meeting seemed liked it had been orchestrated from the start. Marvin said you sabotaged our relationship and wedding. Our meeting at the airport wasn't an accident, was it?"

My heart raced. Was Andrasi a psychopath? He smiled, a cold look pooling in the depths of his cold dark eyes.

"It was love at first sight. If you had been with a better man, then maybe, I might have left the situation alone. But even I could see you were too good for him."

"So you set out to destroy our lives?"

"I rescued you from a potential cheater. He didn't appreciate you. I saw the way he leered at other women, listened to his locker room talk, so I used it against him. He didn't deserve you. So I did some homework and found an ex-girlfriend. One, he couldn't seem to get over."

"Shame on you," I spat. "How dare you play God with our lives."

"You were happier with me, Selena. Our child was meant to be."

As angry as I was, I agreed. I was happier with Andrasi in the short time we were together, than I was during my entire three years with Marvin. And what about our child? He or she wouldn't be here.

"And what about his company? You ruined him."

"As punishment for breaking your heart," Andrasi replied.

"Which you instigated!" I said. "Weren't you friends?"

"Alls fair in love and war. I merely laid the groundwork. A better man would have resisted temptation and showed appreciation for his beautiful bride. Marvin would have cheated on you someday. It was inevitable. I spared you the future misery of marrying a man like him."

"It wasn't your decision to make," I exclaimed. "You said you would never lie to me again, not even by omission."

"We also agreed to leave all past mistakes behind us and start anew. Did we not?"

"Technically, yes. But that was before I knew the truth."

"What truth?" he asked, gazing passionately into my eyes. "That I'm in love in with you?"

He reached into his pocket and dropped to his knee.

"Even though, we are technically, already married by Capa law. I must ask…will you marry me?"

"A few months ago, the answer would have been a resounding yes… but I don't know if I can trust you. You're scary and calculating."

He drew me into his arms and kissed me.

"You are already my wife, will you marry me? I will never betray you. I will never lie to you, not even by omission, ever again, past or present. I need to have you in my life, Selena. I must confess to one more truth to prove I will always be honest with you."

"Of course."

"The people who collected you from your apartment weren't' exactly from immigration, the FBI, or your police department. I hired them to collect you and bring you to my plane."

I stared at him...stunned. "So you tricked me. Why are you so…"

"Infatuated with you? I don't know. It's inexplicable. I just love you. Isn't that enough?"

"It's weird. It's terrifying." I thought, realizing the breadth of Andrasi's planning and deception.

"I won't terrify you. I promise to be a good husband. I just want you back in Capa with me."

I sighed.

"If you promise to not to lie or use your power to get what you want..." I mumbled, still unsure.

"I'm the crown prince. I'm in a position of power, that can't be helped. But with you by my side, I'm already a better man…husband and now a father-to-be. You made me an honest man. I want to be a better man when I am with you."

"What about your mother? She hates me."

"My mother adores you. You are carrying her first grandchild and heir to the throne."

I wasn't sure if I believed him about his mother. I gave a reluctant sigh.

"Yes, I will marry you, Andrasi," I answered.

"Then you have made me the happiest man alive."

It was a fairytale. Ordinary girl meets handsome prince.

Andrasi climbed in bed then drew me into the nook of his arms. "Looks like we have some catching up to do," he smiled.

"We already had our honeymoon," I replied. Andrasi laughed, his eyes overflowing with emotion and love.

--- The End

***Disappear, Love by* E. Hughes**

(Excerpt/Sneak Peek – on sale now)

O inhaled, blowing a ring of smoke out of his mouth. Then he stared at the floor as if deep in thought.

"A little more than a year and a half ago, I was in a car accident. My fiancé died a week before the wedding. I was driving. I don't think he'll ever forgive me. He won't let me move on without him."

"Was your fiancé an unforgiving man?"

"No. He was a good person. He deserves to be here. Me? I'm not so sure about."

My eyes dropped.

"If your fiancé was a good man, he wouldn't want you to be miserable without him. He'd want you to be happy."

"Then why is he in our house?"

"I don't know. The energy in that place is intense. But I don't think it's your fiancé."

"You think I'm crazy, don't you?"

O dumped his cigarette into an ash tray then flipped a mattress from out of the sofa bed.

"Why were you at my house tonight?"

"I came to see you."

"Well obviously…" I answered.

"I couldn't talk to you at the restaurant."

"Why?"

He shook his head. *The walls were up again.*

"I tried talking to you the other night. After we closed the restaurant I rode my bike to your house. I saw you on the bike trail. I called your name but you ran away."

"That was *you*?"

"Who did you think it was? *A ghost*?"

"Don't patronize me, O. You don't know how it feels to lose someone close to you."

"I know exactly how it feels," he answered bitterly.

www.ingramcontent.com/pod-product-compliance
Lightning Source LLC
Chambersburg PA
CBHW030145010826
48973CB00002B/740

* 9 7 8 1 9 6 1 8 2 3 1 0 5 *